Meet the Fortunes—three generations of a family with a legacy of wealth, influence and power. As they gather for a host of weddings, passionate new romances are ignited…and shocking family secrets are revealed…

GRAY McGUIRE: This powerful tycoon is waging his biggest—and most scandalous—battle yet to avenge his father's death. But will his victory cost him the only woman he's ever loved?

MOLLIE SHAW: Mollie Shaw *Fortune?* Almost overnight, this sweet innocent is swept up into a glamorous world. But Mollie already has all she could want. Doesn't she?

CHLOE FORTUNE: Her wedding's just around the corner, but this debutante doesn't look or act like a happy bride-to-be. Still, if there's any man who can win the heart of even the most reluctant bride, it's her handsome groom—Mason Chandler.

Fortune Family Tree

Caleb Fortune* m. Lilah Dulaine

Stuart Fortune m. Marie Smith

[2] GARRETT Fortune
--m.--
Renee Riley

[3] JACK Fortune
--1st m.--
Sandra Alexander (d)
--b--
Lily Fortune
--2nd m.--
Amanda Corbain

[4] MOLLIE SHAW**
--m.--
Gray McGuire

Emmet Fortune m. Annie Mackenzie (d)

[1] MACKENZIE Fortune
--m.--
Kelly Sinclair

Chad Fortune

[5] CHLOE Fortune

Key:
[1] The Honour-Bound Groom
[2] Society Bride
[3] The Secretary and the Millionaire
[4] The Groom's Revenge
[5] Undercover Groom

Symbols:
- - - -   Affair
{   Twins
*   Kate Fortune's brother-in-law
**   Child of Affair

Fortune's Children™
BRIDES

THE GROOM'S REVENGE
Susan Crosby

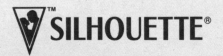

™ SILHOUETTE®

*First published in Great Britain 2000
Silhouette Books, Eton House, 18-24 Paradise Road,
Richmond, Surrey TW9 1SR*

© Harlequin Books S.A. 1999

Special thanks and acknowledgement to
Susan Crosby for her contribution to the
FORTUNE'S CHILDREN: THE BRIDES series.

ISBN 0 373 76214 3

26-0006

*Printed and bound in Spain
by Litografia Rosés S.A., Barcelona*

For Leslie, daughter of my heart, for the joy, love and
friendship you give so passionately.
Kevin must have caught the leprechaun.

SUSAN CROSBY

believes in the value of setting goals, but also in the
magic of making wishes.

Susan earned a B.A. in English while raising her sons,
now grown. She and her husband live in the central valley of California, the land of grapes, asparagus and
almonds. Her chequered past includes jobs as a syn-
chronised swimming instructor, personnel interviewer
at a toy factory and trucking company manager, but her
current occupation as writer is her all-time favourite.

Readers are welcome to write to her at P.O. Box 1836,
Lodi, CA 95241, USA.

Silhouette® is proud to present

**Meet the Fortune brides: special women
who perpetuate a family legacy greater
than mere riches!**

April 2000
A FORTUNE'S CHILDREN WEDDING:
THE HOODWINKED BRIDE
Barbara Boswell

THE HONOUR-BOUND GROOM
Jennifer Greene

May 2000
SOCIETY BRIDE
Elizabeth Bevarly

THE SECRETARY AND THE MILLIONAIRE
Leanne Banks

June 2000
THE GROOM'S REVENGE
Susan Crosby

UNDERCOVER GROOM
Merline Lovelace

**Remember, where there's a bride…
there's a *wedding!***

One

A leprechaun winked at Gray McGuire as he entered the quaint little Minneapolis flower shop—his second clue that this day would be different from any other.

Stopping mid-stride, he crouched in front of the foot-tall, molded-plastic creature that propped open the door of Every Bloomin' Thing. Battery operated? he wondered.

"Top o' the mornin' to ye," the creature shrieked.

Gray examined it more closely. Motion sensor?

"Top o' the afternoon to you, Yarg!" a woman called from somewhere in the shop.

Scrutinizing the creature again, Gray waited for the elf to answer her. The whimsical notion caught him off guard, yet there was something about this place that lent itself to whimsy.

He looked around as he stood. Even with the door open, the shop smelled fragrant and exotic, a mix of oxygen-heavy scents. Moisture-laden air cooled his skin, warm from his having stood a long while in the late-July sun as he'd watched the shop.

No one had come or gone in the time he'd observed the tiny storefront tucked into the well-tended, older neighborhood. Hoping that meant Mollie Shaw, the shop owner, was alone, he'd finally crossed the street, anticipation churning inside him—his first clue that the day would be different.

Anxiety was foreign to him. He studied. He analyzed. He planned.

And he didn't like the unfamiliar edginess now, so he took another minute to relax before he made his presence known, even though a sign on the counter invited him to ring the bell for service. A brass bell with a fairy creature perched on the tip of the handle.

"So, what do you think?"

He sought the source of the disembodied voice, wondering if the woman could see him even though he couldn't see her. The shop seemed magical, after all.

"I think it'll make men look twice, don't you?"

The woman was batty, Gray decided. No one answered her, and she certainly wasn't talking to him.

"Of course I'm right," she said.

He had to see this woman who talked to herself. Stepping silently around the counter he spied her attempting to shove an oak credenza along the floor. She seemed familiar, although she shouldn't. He purposely hadn't tracked down a photograph of her—which was out of character for him. Details were his life. He'd balked, however, at seeing her image ahead of time, this woman whose life he was about to change.

Who did she remind him of…?

Cinderella! Mollie Shaw—if indeed, this was she—looked like Cinderella. Her long hair was a rich coppery red instead of blond like the Disney movie character, but she wore a small, triangular scarf over it, keeping her hair out of her face. Her pale green blouse and snug jeans sported streaks of dirt. He admired the picture she made from behind as she shoved again, her breath expelling with the effort.

"If Tony doesn't get here soon, I'm going to pass out," she muttered.

"Where do you want it?" Gray asked, coming up beside her.

Her eyes widened, eyes the color of a deep, dark forest, where mysteries beckoned. Where leprechauns might play— He dismissed the fanciful thought as he watched her reaction. She took a step back, not answering him, her lips parted. He couldn't read her expression. Fear? He'd come upon her without warning, after all.

"You're...you're—" She stopped, seeming to catch her breath. "I can't believe it."

"I'm Gray McGuire."

"I know. I saw you on CNN yesterday."

His gaze strayed to a little smudge of dirt at the corner of her mouth and lingered until her words registered. She knew him? He shouldered her aside, deciding that her knowing could only help his cause. She would probably trust him sooner. "Just point out where you want this thing."

She pointed.

He almost laughed. Then he muscled the credenza where she indicated.

"There's more." She gestured to a bookcase-type piece. "It goes on top. It's a hutch. If you'll grab one side, I'll take the..."

Her voice faded as he lifted the piece, then set it where it belonged. When he turned around he caught her sliding the scarf from her hair.

"Thanks," she said, jamming the fabric into her back pocket. "I'm Mollie Shaw."

She didn't extend her hand, so he did. She hesitated, then finally rubbed her palm along her thigh before shaking his hand.

He knew she was twenty-two, which suddenly seemed decades younger than his thirty-three. He judged her height to be about eight inches shorter than his six foot one, her build as slight as the fairy on top of the bell. The bones of her hand were delicate, the flesh unpampered.

And she seemed a little starstruck, of all things, which could complicate his plans. He intended to propose a partnership with her, one completely unrelated to either her business or his. They would need a professional relationship.

She glanced over her shoulder. Tension radiated from her. When she looked at him again, she smiled, but a smile mixed with—what? Embarrassment? She pulled him around the hutch and into the main section of the shop before she let go of his hand.

"You caught me redecorating," she said. "I've been putting it off for months."

Probably eight months, he thought. Since her mother died.

"Wednesdays are slow," she hurried on. "I should've waited for my helper to get here. But once I got going, I didn't want to stop."

"What are you going to put in the hutch that will make men look twice?" he asked.

"Um, you heard that, did you?"

She wiped a finger along the counter without leaving a mark. No dust settled in this hardworking woman's domain.

"Men tend to spend more than women do," she said as if sharing a secret with him. "Sometimes they want something in addition to flowers, so I thought I'd start carrying some jewelry, too. Maybe some perfume. Pottery might sell well. One-stop shopping for the man who wants to appear romantic but who actually waited until the last minute."

Or a man who's hiding a guilty conscience, Gray thought.

He wondered whether her redecorating was the result of coming out of mourning for her mother or financial need. In a shop this size, she must barely eke out a living, he decided, anger brewing at the unfairness. She shouldn't have to live like this. It was a wrong Gray intended to right—with her help—as well as fixing what had been wrong in his own life for twenty-five years.

"Your initial investment could be substantial, and slow to bring returns," he said, protective of her but not questioning why. He knew why.

Mollie eyed the empty hutch. "Too much, do you think?" she asked, looking around and sighing, something she'd been doing a lot lately. "Things haven't changed around here in a long, long time. I want to drum up some new business, but I can't afford to take any losses."

"You should discuss this with your business manager."

"Um, I'll do that." She dragged her tongue along the inside of her cheek.

"You don't have a business manager," he said, awareness in his eyes.

She shook her head, a smile tugging at her mouth. *No one will ever believe me,* she thought. Gray McGuire, the high-tech wizard from the Silicon Valley was here. In her shop. He'd materialized from her dreams and was actually talking to her. He'd touched her. *Touched* her.

"Tax accountant?" he asked hopefully.

"I'm sort of a full-service shop owner."

He was even more attractive in person than in any photo she'd seen. Clipped. Saved.

His blue eyes were startling against his California tan, his dark brown hair shiny and thick. She'd admired the sculpted muscles of his arms when he'd lifted the hutch top onto the credenza as if it weighed no more than a wicker basket. The turquoise polo shirt and khaki pants he wore fit his body perfectly, showing off a well-toned physique, one that didn't look like he spent his days behind a desk.

He was *here.* In *her* shop. *Gray McGuire.*

"I apologize," he said, moving around the shop, looking at the merchandise. "You weren't asking my advice."

"I always listen to advice." Standing in front of the counter, her hands clasped, she was content to watch him, afraid if she did something wrong, he would disappear in a puff of smoke.

He must think her crazy the way she was talking to him as if she'd known him forever. But, in truth, she felt she had. Although he lived in California, his photograph had been in the *StarTribune* following a gala charity event attended by the city's most prominent family—the Fortunes—a month ago, and he often graced the pages of *Time, Newsweek* and the like.

Her obsession had begun harmlessly enough. She had made a completely innocent comment to her new acquaintances Amanda and Chloe Fortune upon seeing his picture in the newspaper—a comment along the lines of Mollie wishing that someone like Gray McGuire would sweep her off her feet. Amanda had promptly ripped out the picture and told Mollie to sleep on it, and maybe he would be hers.

Mollie had laughed at the joke, but kept the photo. After

months of mourning her mother's death, she'd found a new focus, something to think about other than relentless grief and loneliness. And after too many nights of dreamless sleep, she started dreaming again. So Mollie had read everything she could get her hands on about Gray McGuire, fixating on him because it made her feel alive again.

It didn't even make sense that she was fascinated by a man who was the CEO of a software design and manufacturing company, McGuire Enterprises. A man who'd designed a computer operating system at age twenty. A man who spoke to Congress on computer security issues. He'd lunched with the president yesterday!

And if he'd caught a glimpse of that newspaper picture of him she'd taped under her counter, he would have hightailed it out of there faster than she could say, "You're the man of my dreams. Literally." She'd even been talking to his picture when he'd arrived.

She continued to wait as he set some wind chimes moving, then listened to the tinkling sounds. He dipped a finger into the recirculating pond that kept the moisture content of the room high, the bubbles more soothing than music. He sniffed a few of the potted plants, studied the markers, printed with the plant name and care instructions, that were jammed into each pot.

She didn't want to hurry him, but she was more than a little curious about why he was there. Well, technically she was flabbergasted. But she was really, really curious. If this were a fairy tale, he'd be pulling a glass slipper out of his pocket about now and trying it on her foot—and it would fit.

"It's a nice shop," he said at last. "You're also a wedding planner."

"How do you know that?"

He pointed to the left. "There's a sign in your window."

"Oh." She smiled, feeling a little sheepish. She'd thought maybe he was her soul mate, after all—that he could read her mind.

"If you call yourself a consultant, not only would you be following the current market trend, you could probably charge a higher fee."

"Why would I want to do that? My fees are reasonable. Anyway, I'm just getting started. You know the Fortune family, right? I've heard them speak of you."

He returned to her side, his expression impassive. "You're friends with the Fortunes?"

He stood so close she could touch him if she wanted. His clean, soapy scent made her nose twitch. "My good friend Kelly married Mac Fortune, and I pulled the event together for them. Then I was invited to do Mac's sister Chloe's wedding to Mason Chandler in a few months. One of those fairy-tale-princess weddings, with all the trimmings."

"The kind of wedding you'd like for yourself?"

She shrugged. "It's fun to plan."

"But?"

"It wouldn't be in my budget."

Matter-of-fact words, Gray noted. "Your parents wouldn't help?" he asked, surprised at her candor. People didn't usually open up so easily to him. It was the magic of this shop, he decided. And this fairy-sprite woman.

"My father's been gone since before I was born. My mother passed away late last year."

She crouched in front of a flowering plant, seeming to inspect it for insects or dead leaves or something. He zeroed in on the scarf she'd tucked into her pocket, then was distracted by the distinctly feminine curve of her rear.

He lifted his gaze in a flash when her words registered. Been gone? What did that mean? Did she think her father was dead? "I'm sorry."

"Thank you. Now," she glanced up at him. "What can I do for you, Mr. McGuire?"

"First, you can call me Gray. I'm a little surprised you know me."

She fussed with another plant. "The Fortunes have spoken of you."

"But you recognized my face."

"I told you. I saw you on the news yesterday."

"Hey, Mol! Sorry I'm late."

A young man swooped into the shop, Minnesota Twins cap

on his head, baseball glove tucked under his arm. He was sixteen or seventeen, Gray decided, and into body building.

"What a game! Man, we destroyed 'em." His gaze landed on Gray. "Hey, you're that guy—"

"Gray McGuire," Mollie said instantly, moving to stand between them, putting her back to Gray.

"Yeah, I know. He's—"

"In town," she interrupted. "Say hello, then get to the deliveries, okay, Tony?"

He knows who I am, too? Confused, Gray eyed the back of Mollie's head. This was getting weird. Computers must be a passion of hers. Why else would she know of him?

Tony frowned. "What about the stuff you wanted me to move?"

"Later." She grabbed his arm, pulling him along with her to a refrigerated case, housing cut flowers. "Those two boxes and the mixed bouquet there."

"Okay." As he took the items from the refrigerator, he spoke over his shoulder to Gray. "I've been trying to convince her to get with the times, you know? Get a computer? Maybe you can talk her into it."

"I thought you liked working here," Mollie said, exasperation in her voice.

He grinned. "All bark," he said to Gray, then he headed out the door, his arms full.

Gray was more confused than ever. "Your business isn't computerized?" he asked her when they were alone.

"No." She moved around the counter, leaving a trail of scent. Something subtle. Elusive. A four-leaf clover—

"Computers terrify me," she said.

"You'd get comfortable soon enough."

She crossed her arms. "They crash. They lose crucial information. They make people tear out their hair. Why would I put myself through that?"

"Convenience."

Mollie smiled at his droll tone.

"Top of the mornin' to ye!"

The leprechaun's shriek brought a return of normalcy to Mollie's afternoon. Yarg shouted a greeting every twenty minutes, which meant that Gray McGuire had been in her shop for that long, and she still didn't know why.

"I'm assuming Computerphobics Anonymous didn't send you my way," she said to him. "What brings you to Every Bloomin' Thing?"

"I have a proposition for you."

Mollie felt her face heat at the images his simple statement conjured up. A proposition? One involving getting naked? Her dreams about him were romantic, not sexual—declarations of his undying devotion and a chaste, pure love. Certainly nothing physical…even if he did have a body that made her take more than a second glance.

"I hope I'm misunderstanding your meaning." Shocked at herself, she felt a flush spread across her face. Of all the stupid things to say to him. Of course he wasn't interested in her—not in that way. How foolish could she be?

"Strictly business," he said gently, making her feel even worse. He must think her so naive.

"Oh, Mollie, dear!"

Mollie stifled a groan as a tiny, white-haired woman marched past the leprechaun doorman and into the shop, her heels clicking on the linoleum floor. She nodded at Gray.

"Good afternoon, Mrs. Bauer," Mollie said after sending an apologetic look in Gray's direction. At this rate she would never find out why he was here. "What can I do for you?"

"Reverend Kruger is ill."

"I hope it's not too serious."

"Serious enough that we will have a substitute this week. Reverend Schmidt. He's allergic to stock."

Gray listened to the exchange between the women as they discussed alternatives, deciding that "stock" was a flower that Mollie used in the floral arrangements she did for the church on Sunday. That revelation made him reconsider how much to involve her in his plans. He'd intended to align himself with her against Stuart Fortune. But the young woman who was afraid of computers, charged reasonable rates and made flower arrangements for Sunday morning worship, lived in a sheltered world that could not possibly have prepared her for launching a vendetta that would turn her into a media darling, especially one born of an old scandal he would bring to light.

Mollie Shaw was a crucial component of Gray's plan to make Stuart Fortune's indiscretions and thievery public. But now that Gray had met this innocent young woman, how could he involve her?

How can you not? Justice must be rendered.

"I'm sorry for the interruption," Mollie said.

He looked around. They were alone again.

"You have a proposition for me?" she prompted him.

He had to rethink this. "I have to go. I'm expected somewhere else in a few minutes," he said, glancing at his watch, then heading for the door.

"Will you be back?"

Her words stopped him. There was something in her voice. A hopefulness he couldn't ignore. He didn't know what would happen next. He had to analyze—

"Please do come again," she said softly.

He should resist the temptation of her vulnerability, which whispered to his conscience first, then somewhere deeper, bringing light into the darkness of his plans, his need for vengeance. Instead he said, "I'll be in touch," over his shoulder as he moved toward the door again.

Not wanting his last image to be of the fairylike Mollie Shaw, he looked at the leprechaun instead. He knew it had to be his imagination, but the elf seemed to smile with approval.

Stuart Fortune's Twin Cities-based company, Knight Star Systems, occupied fifty acres of prime industrial property. The gated compound was ordinary—a large factory building with a parking lot to the west, receiving dock on the south and corporate offices attached to the north end. Knight Star Systems designed, manufactured and installed security systems for automobiles, homes, office buildings, hotels, airports, even sports arenas. Large commercial accounts made up more and more of their customer base each year.

Gray parked where he could watch the office employees exit.

He glanced at his watch. Just a few minutes more. Stuart followed an unvarying routine. On Mondays he worked in the Fortune Corporation offices. The rest of the workweek he spent here, always the last to leave the office each day, although the factory hummed through the night. Three times a year they shut down for plant-wide vacations, each lasting a week.

It was a streamlined and successful operation—until recently. Small setbacks had compounded. Soon the struggle to keep their edge in the highly competitive market would impact the entire operation.

No one would have guessed Gray had choreographed the shocking downfall. He had moved slowly toward his goal, letting Stuart wonder, then worry. Panic would follow before long.

Gray sat up a little straighter as Stuart exited the building, a tall, fit man with a confident gait. His temples were dusted with gray; a few lines fanned from his eyes. Otherwise he didn't appear fifty-five, much less the sixty-two he really was.

He shouldn't look that good. That healthy. That happy.

He should look like a man with blood on his hands.

My father's blood.

Gray's jaw ached as he watched Stuart unlock his just-off-the-lot Cadillac, toss his briefcase and suit jacket onto the passenger seat, then slip behind the wheel. Within seconds he passed through the front gate, turned right and headed toward his home by the lake, a two-story stone structure with picturesque views from every window, a gated entrance, paved-brick driveway and six-car garage.

The trappings of success. How little they mattered in the end. What mattered to Gray was justice, Knight Star Systems, and now, Mollie Shaw, fellow victim. Stuart's sons had grown up with every possible luxury, while his daughter deliberated about spending a couple thousand dollars to improve her business. The injustice burned like acid in Gray's gut. Stuart had gotten away with too much for too long. His reign had to end. And Gray intended to end it—for his own peace of mind. And Mollie's.

She deserved to know the truth, especially now that she was alone and struggling to stay afloat. Gray would force retribution—the financial settlement she deserved. It would help to balance the scales.

Mollie would be free of money problems.

Gray would be free. Free.

People would be hurt—like he'd been hurt. But he had recovered and moved on. So would they.

Mollie peeled the tape from Gray's newspaper photo then slid the yellowing scrap into a folder of invoices hand-stamped Paid. The thought of his picture nestled within her uncomputerized paperwork appealed to her. Before she shut the folder she leaned her elbows on the counter and studied him, so elegant in his stylish tuxedo. He wasn't even wearing a bow tie, but one of those collarless shirts not requiring a tie at all.

Something about him made her mouth water. Maybe it was his posture, which was perfect. Perhaps it was his hair, which invited a woman's caress. Or his jaw, strong and oh, so masculine. He was infinitely touchable.

Unfolding the paper to reveal the half she usually kept turned to the back, she examined the whole photograph. Maybe what she liked most was the way he seemed to totally ignore the woman whose arm was tucked through his as if she owned him, whose breast pressed against him like an engraved invitation. Mollie hated her—Samantha Simeon, the caption said, someone whose path would not likely cross Mollie's.

But then, she wouldn't have imagined her path crossing Gray McGuire's, either.

With a sigh she put away the folder, then locked the front and back doors before turning out the lights and climbing the stairs to her apartment above the shop. Her quiet, lonely apartment.

She'd lived there all her life, had never had the slightest interest in finding her own place after she graduated from high school. Her mother, Karen, had been her best friend as well as the only family she had. Their lives had been completely intertwined, and Mollie missed her desperately.

Maybe she should have developed more friendships through the years, but she'd been happy in her mother's company—and

Karen hadn't pushed. She'd even seemed to encourage Mollie to stay home rather than going out much.

Which made Karen's unexpected death so much harder to take. The only good thing to happen since was Kelly's marriage to Mac Fortune, which gave Mollie a connection with the illustrious Fortune family that she'd never dared to dream about, although that relationship was more business than social, so far.

Into this rather bewildering new life had come Gray McGuire. Not by accident, either, but because he had a business proposition for her. What in the world could he possibly want?

She should call Kelly. Maybe Mac knew what Gray wanted. Perhaps he had even recommended her shop. Of course! That was it. Mac or one of the other Fortunes had recommended her for…for…something.

Mollie stared into her refrigerator and saw nothing that interested her, so she tucked her keys and a few dollars into her pocket then skipped down the stairs to enjoy the summer evening before the sun went down.

She stopped to buy a peach frozen yogurt then continued down the block to a park where she'd played as a child. Settling on a bench, she savored her dessert-for-dinner treat as children played. The familiarity inevitably brought back memories.

It was in this park that she'd learned of her mother's dark, painful secrets. If Karen had lived longer, would she have confided in her daughter about her life before Mollie was born—and her controlling, eventually abusive husband?

Karen had kept that part of her life secret, writing the details in her journals, instead, which Mollie found soon after her death. Mollie had taken the treasures with her to this very park to read her mother's life story, expecting an entertaining tale, discovering tragedy instead.

And triumph. Karen had shielded her—perhaps too much— because of her past and because she'd had to be mother and father, nurturer and provider.

Mollie scraped the last of the yogurt from the cup, scraping the memories away, as well. If Karen were there, she would tell her daughter that she'd mourned long enough. That life was short. That when an interesting man like Gray McGuire appeared out of nowhere—and could drop out of sight just as easily—she shouldn't wait for him to make all the moves.

Except—what did Mollie know about "moves"? And interesting men? Regardless of the fact Minneapolis wasn't a small town, she was a small-town girl with uncomplicated needs.

But, ever hopeful, Mollie figured tomorrow she would wear that pretty lilac dress she'd found last week marked down for the third time, bringing it into her price range. She could dust on some powder, add a dab or two of matching perfume. Perhaps even a little mascara. No blush, though. He brought color to her cheeks easily enough already.

It was a business proposition, after all, no matter what her hormones were singing in multipart harmony to the contrary.

Two

_____

Although her heart rate zoomed from a waltz tempo to a thundering hard-rock beat, Mollie continued to fill a round vase with summer flowers as she watched Gray approach her shop around noon the next day. Daisy petals quivered as she slid the bloom amongst the others, her hands shaking. Last night she'd prowled her apartment until midnight, watched an old movie that made her cry, then finally fell asleep on the sofa. Her normally hazy, romantic dreams of Gray had been replaced with sharp, vivid images of him in the flesh.

He crossed the threshold, eyeing Yarg as he entered. His blue jeans showed off narrow hips and long legs. His baby blue T-shirt didn't fit like a second skin, but didn't mask his muscular torso, either. She pursed her lips, trapping an admiring sigh.

"Good day, Miss Shaw," he said as he reached the counter.

"Top o' the mornin' to ye!"

Mollie's gaze flickered to the screeching leprechaun. "And from Yarg and myself, Mr. McGuire."

"Is there a volume control on that thing?"

"Just an on-off switch. I guess I've gotten used to it." She wondered whether Gray's real-life kissing technique would do justice to her dreams. Could anyone compete with a dream? "I hope you've come to put me out of my misery."

"Did the suspense get to you?"

"I'm not too good at delayed gratification," she said, openly flirting with him, trying to get a response. Instead he walked to the front window and stared outside, ignoring her.

Chagrined, she held her ground. Late last night she'd reread all the articles she'd saved about him. While he spoke freely about his work and vision, his personal life was apparently taboo. Speculation abounded, fueled only by brief quotes from women he'd allegedly dated. Some called him distracted and distinctly unromantic, one woman went so far as to brand him as "cold."

Which apparently hadn't stopped the woman from dating him more than once. Mollie wouldn't call him cold. Steady, perhaps. Not given to mood swings. And the allegation about not being romantic…was probably true. She figured his mind was a minicomputer in which he probably maintained a mental agenda. Mollie was apparently an item on that list, and he would get to her in his own time.

He seemed to jar himself back into awareness as a dark-haired man wearing a brown delivery uniform breezed into the shop carrying a large box. "Hey, Mollie. I see you've joined the twentieth century just in time for the twenty-first."

"What kind of riddle is that, Mike?"

He set the package on the floor beside the counter. "Your computer."

"Computer? Me? I didn't—" She narrowed her eyes at Gray, who leaned an elbow against the countertop and watched her impassively. "There's been a mistake. You can load it right back on the truck."

"There's no mistake. I'll be back with the rest of the stuff in a minute. You'll need to sign for 'em."

She waited until Mike climbed back into his truck, then she planted her fists on her hips. "That's your company logo on the box," she said after studying the package.

"I believe you're right."

"I can't accept that kind of gift."

"Did I say it was a gift?"

She sputtered. He expected her to pay for something she hadn't ordered? And didn't want? This was not the man of her dreams. Not even close. That man respected her, acknowledged her as an intelligent and independent person and admired her business sense. But the man standing in front of her had decided after a half-hour conversation that he knew her well enough to tell her how to run her business.

"I can't pay for this," she said, forcing the words out.

"I don't send a computer unsolicited, then expect someone to pay for it, Mollie."

"But you said it wasn't a gift."

"It isn't."

"Well. That's crystal clear."

Gray enjoyed her temper, bright as a newly minted penny. "Sign for the delivery and I'll explain."

"I'll just be calling in a pickup order for tomorrow."

"That'll be your decision. For now, just accept it. Please," he said. Mike returned in time to overhear their discussion.

She cursed Gray with her eyes but scrawled her name across the signature pad when Mike slid it across the counter, grinning.

"He won't keep his mouth shut," she almost growled when they were alone again. "Everyone up and down the block will know."

"I wasn't the one making a fuss," Gray said mildly.

"I would expect a man like you to get to the point," she said through clenched teeth.

"A man like me?"

"Brilliant. Analytical." She frowned. "Although *People* magazine also called you quirky." She lost her fighting edge for a moment as she seemed to think about that.

Had she gone to the library last night and read up on him? He never had figured out why that reporter had labeled him as quirky, a definition Gray would never apply to himself. He'd told her she could ask questions while he jogged his eight miles, because he didn't have time for her otherwise. Did that make him quirky? Or efficient?

"You work hard and you're ambitious," he said to Mollie. "I respect that. You're trying to take what's already a charming little shop and make it more upscale, to attract new business, right?"

"Without losing any of the old customers." Diverted from her argument, she mirrored his pose across the counter, leaning toward him.

"The coffeehouse down the block draws a different crowd into the area," he said.

"There's a lot of revitalization going on here. New businesses are mushrooming. There's a lot of potential business because the neighborhood has changed. I would've moved my business here, if I hadn't already been here."

He nodded. He'd done some quick research on the subject. An infusion of cash would certainly help her give a fresh new look to her shop. "The whole area is on the brink of a renaissance."

"And I want to be ready."

"Then you'll need to computerize your business."

"Why?"

"For one, when you get on the Internet, you can locate other florists and see what they're doing. You won't believe the doors that will open to you."

Interest flashed in her eyes before she clamped her mouth shut and pushed away from the counter. "Why do you care?"

He'd come up with his new plan last night, pleased with his solution. He had to buy himself some time, let her get to know him, then convince her to help him ruin Stuart Fortune. For now, though, he just needed a reason to keep her in close contact.

"I want you to plan my parents' twenty-fifth wedding anniversary party."

Surprise widened her eyes. "Twenty-fifth? But—"

"My mother and stepfather," he said.

"Oh. I guess I assumed they lived in California."

"They do. That's why you'll need a computer."

Mollie frowned. Her world had stopped making sense the moment Gray had dropped into her life, the man who didn't know he'd helped her bury her grief. But not only did his request not make sense, it was downright ridiculous. Not just quirky. *Ridiculous.* Absurd. Preposterous.

So why did she just want to say okay without questioning his motives? Surely he had motives.

"You must have a choice of a hundred party planners where you live," she said.

"Last month I attended a charity ball here in Minneapolis. You were one of the sponsors."

"How do you know that?"

"I won one of the table centerpieces. A basket decorated with dried flowers. Very original. Your business card was taped to the bottom." He pulled it out of his pocket and showed her. "I shipped the basket to my mother the next day, because I thought it was something she would like. And she did. Obviously you're the right person for the job."

The phone rang. She watched him peel off a packing slip from one of the computer boxes as she handled a frantic caller requesting a dozen long-stemmed red roses for a just-remembered anniversary. Yes, she had some on hand, she told the man with the stress-filled voice. Yes, roses were expensive, but his wife was priceless, wasn't she? Yes, she took Mastercard. Yes, he could pick them up in half an hour.

Gray looked at his watch no less than five times in the few minutes she was on the phone.

After she hung up she moved to the refrigerator case and lifted out a tall vase filled with roses, then grabbed some baby's breath, lemon leaves and leather fern.

She lined a long gold-foil box with forest green tissue paper, a task that soothed her with its familiarity. In a world turned upside down, she needed routine. "Why me?" she asked.

"Because I've seen and admired your work, as I said. And because you're from home."

"Here?" She'd stripped the lower stems of thorns and leaves before putting them in the refrigerator. Grabbing her paring knife, she made an angle cut at the bottom of each stem before sliding it into a water-filled tube. Gray wandered close to watch.

"My mother and stepfather were born in Minneapolis," he said, his gaze following her hands as she worked. "So was I."

"I didn't know that."

"Is there a reason why you should?"

She layered roses, greenery and baby's breath in the box. "I suppose not. I'm just surprised. Still, that's hardly enough reason to put me in charge of a party that will take place so far from here. It's not practical. Or are you planning to have the party here?"

"No. It'll be near where they live in Atherton. That's in Northern California, near what's called the Silicon Valley. Near Stanford University."

"When?"

"April twentieth."

She dropped the length of ribbon she'd just snipped. "April, as in next year? Nine months from now?"

"Does that give you enough time?"

"Gee, I don't know, Gray. That might be cutting it awfully close." She swiped the ribbon from the floor, then formed a big, loopy, red bow.

"I figured we'd need to reserve the facility well in advance. I expect several hundred people to attend."

"What does it have to do with my having a computer?" she asked, chagrined that he was right.

"It's the best way of staying in touch to handle the details."

She looked up at him for a second, then focused on attaching the ribbon to the box. "You do remember we have telephones here in Minneapolis, right? And fax machines."

"I prefer e-mail."

"You would," she mumbled.

"What was that?"

She could hear the smile in his voice and tried to decide whether she liked being a source of entertainment for him. "I said, 'Oh, good.'"

"Are you interested in handling the party?"

"Of course I'm interested." She set the box of roses in the refrigerator. "It's just that I still can't figure out why you'd use me. I'm new at this, plus the distance."

"You won't grow your business with that attitude."

She laughed. "Grow my business?"

"Standard business terminology," he said, although he smiled.

"I'd have to hire help for the shop."

"Build it into your budget for the job."

"I need to think about this."

He put his hands in his pockets. "There's no time to think about it. I won't be in town for long. I need to set up your computer and teach you the basics before I go."

Mollie skirted around him, deciding she needed the safety of the counter between them. Standing close to him had just made her want to kiss him even more. He had the most appealing mouth....

"I can take computer classes," she said, dragging her invoice pad close and writing up a bill for the roses.

"I want to be the one to teach you."

"Of course you do."

Gray waited until she stopped writing and looked up at him. Had he come on too strong? Had she picked up on the intensity of his pursuit, even as he tried to go slow with her, to be casual? "Do I make you nervous, Mollie? Yesterday you talked to me like an old friend."

"Yesterday you weren't real." She made a little sound, as if regretting her words. "I mean, the situation didn't seem real. Your being here. What are the odds?"

"I already explained that. And you're making this difficult, Mollie Shaw."

Her eyes sparkled at his comment.

"I would've figured you for a man who likes a challenge, Gray McGuire. So, here's the way it'll work. I'll use the computer until the party is over, then if I find I want to keep it, I'll buy it from you."

"At cost."

"Well, of course. By then it'll be a used computer. Hardly worth my paying full price."

The sound of his own laughter surprised him. For a moment he'd forgotten that justice was within his grasp. He had to stay focused on his goal, not be tempted into forgetting his purpose. After all, justice would be hers, too.

"Where can I hook up the computer?" he asked her.

Mollie looked around her work space.

"While you're learning," he said, "your living quarters would probably be best. You can practice without interruptions."

"That would be upstairs. I'll show you the way." She locked the cash register, then moved to the stack of boxes.

"You're going to let me into your apartment? Just like that? When you hardly know me?"

She grabbed the top two boxes, leaving the heavy one for him. "What could I have that you could possibly want?"

As she walked away shaking her head, he studied her long, shiny hair and slender back, her softly swaying skirt, envisioning the lithe body beneath it. A drift of something in the air had him breathing deeply. A rainbow would smell like that. Frowning at the thought, he followed her trail through the back of the shop and up the stairs to a small, neat apartment with a distinctly floral motif. Femininity personified.

After Mollie made a quick return to the shop, Gray surveyed the apartment. The first door led to a bedroom. Twin beds. She must have shared the room with her mother, a situation not conducive to romantic liaisons, for either of them.

One wall was dotted with framed photographs of Mollie and her mother through the years. He studied each picture, noting the same wide, smiling mouths and reed-slender bodies, the deep-copper-colored hair. The togetherness.

He wandered out of the bedroom and into the bathroom, with its claw-foot tub and garden-print shower curtain. The room smelled of woman, something flowery and fragrant and... comforting.

Comfort. Something he neither wanted nor needed. *Be a man.* His stepfather's words echoed in Gray's mind, as they had since the day his mother had married James McGuire when Gray was eight. No allowance for weakness. No quarter given. Go after what you want, no matter the cost. Winner takes all. Losers...die.

James McGuire was a winner. Stuart Fortune was a winner. Gray's father...

Go after what you want, Gray reminded himself as he returned to the living room to unbox the computer components. Along a wall, desk space had been created by laying a Formica counter-top on two-drawer file cabinets, making room for two people to work simultaneously. He chose the side closest to the phone jack, wondering how much of a fuss Mollie was going to put up at having a second line installed. For now he would set up the modem on her existing line. He hooked up the hard drive, the monitor, the printer. He loaded software, including an Inter-net server.

All the while he eyed a cigar box bearing Mollie's name in bright purple paint over a crudely designed birthday cake and candles made of sequins and glitter. It looked like something a very young child might have done as a school project.

Gray glanced toward the open front door. Mollie's voice drifted up the stairwell from the shop. With just his forefinger he lifted the lid of the decorated cigar box. He leaned closer, seeing birthday-cake candles inside. A piece of paper was taped to each—

"Gray!"

Plunk. The lip dropped into place. He put his fingers on the keyboard at the sound of Mollie hurrying up the stairs.

"Hi," she said breathlessly as she came up beside him. "Wow. You've got it all set up and going."

"Just testing it out."

"It looks confusing."

"Pretty soon it won't. Did you want something?"

She curved her hand over his shoulder and bent low to look at the screen with him. Her fragrance—heather?—dropped a net over him so that he couldn't move, could barely breathe. Like some damned teenager, he thought, amazed. Heat flashed through him.

"What's that?" she asked.

"E-mail from my office."

"You can get mail on my computer?"

"I set you up with the same server." He turned his head fractionally toward her. "Did you come up here for something in particular?"

She moved a little closer to him. "You seem a little warm."

Warm, hell. His blood had begun to simmer.

She straightened. "Do you need the air-conditioning turned up?"

"I'm comfortable, Mollie. Is that all?" *Move away.*

"Did you want something to eat or drink? Tony's here. He can get something from the coffeehouse. There's not much in my refrigerator."

He'd noticed. A pitcher of iced tea, two peaches, milk, several cartons of yogurt. A couple of unidentifiable items in plastic containers.

And a red-velvet, heart-shaped box of candy, half-full.

He glanced at his watch. "I'm fine for now. Why don't I just order some takeout to be delivered around the time the shop closes? We can eat together, then get to work showing you how this computer is going to simplify your life."

"Okay. If it's pizza, I don't like mushrooms."

"Any other likes or dislikes?" He saw her glance settle on the cigar box.

Her cheeks flushed. Casually she swept up the box, tucking it close to her chest. "Not really," she said.

"Are you adventurous?"

Mollie shrugged, letting him choose his own answer from the vague gesture. Adventurous? Hardly. More like "tiresomely sensible." Except that less than a minute ago she'd almost pressed her lips to his. She wondered what he would have thought of that, considering his claim that everything was to be strictly business between them.

"Any particular wine you like?" he asked.

She shook her head. She'd had maybe five glasses of wine in her whole life. The box she clutched seemed to weigh a ton. Had he looked inside? Were her secrets no longer secrets? She must have been really nervous not to notice the box sitting out when she'd first brought him upstairs. She'd gotten used to it being there over the past several months, since her last birthday—the day she'd stopped believing in making wishes. She'd been working up the nerve to throw the box into the trash.

"I need to get back to work," she said, aware of his watchful silence.

She hurried into the bedroom and shoved the box into a drawer, sliding it under her lingerie, a fancy name for her plain, practical bras and panties. But then, she was a practical person.

Mollie mumbled goodbye as she hurried through the living room and down the stairs, fighting images of Gray seeing just how practical she was. She knew there wasn't a chance in heaven that he would be interested in someone like her, someone so unsophisticated. And computer illiterate—a major strike against her, undoubtedly.

Don't mix business and pleasure. How many times had she heard that? And if she took a chance on letting things become personal between them, then he rejected her, would she lose not only the job, but her dreams? For the past month she'd spun fantasies about him without any fuel other than magazine and newspaper stories and photos.

She needed him to fill up the emptiness. She also wanted to know the real man beneath those glossy pages.

There had to be some reason why she'd chosen him as her obsession when she'd never even had the slightest crush on anyone before, not even a movie star or singer. Gray was a businessman. A genius. An international icon—

Who had the prettiest blue eyes, the nicest smile and the most incredible body she'd ever seen. And for the first time in months, she wasn't lonely.

Three

———

Mollie's mouth caught fire. So much for her first foray into adventure, she thought as she swallowed half a glass of Chardonnay to douse the flames.

Gray had ordered Thai takeout, and while most of it was just a little spicy and really delicious, the chilies in one dish burned her mouth, her throat and anywhere that the fumes alone touched. She didn't care much for his amused smile, or the way he continued to eat the blistering dish as if it were macaroni and cheese.

"You said—" she panted "—it was hot." She took another swig of wine. "But I didn't expect fire. Your taste buds must be cauterized." She took her plate into the kitchen, grabbed a Popsicle from the freezer, then plopped back onto the sofa beside him. She'd already consumed two glasses of wine, and the room seemed draped with gauze.

"It's an acquired taste." He closed the cartons with their leftovers and carried them into the kitchen.

"Grab a Popsicle, if you want," she said, then moaned as the frozen treat numbed her mouth at last.

"I'm okay, thanks," he called out.

She heard water running and realized he was rinsing the dishes, something she should be doing, but nothing could have induced her to put aside her icy first aid. Warm and lazy from the wine, she snuggled into the cushions and closed her eyes.

After a minute she felt him sit beside her.

"Something tells me you aren't exactly ready for computer lessons," he said, humor in his voice.

"Whose fault is that?"

"I didn't know that two glasses of wine would put you under."

"Now you know." She opened her eyes and smiled at him.

"Your lips are red."

"Cherry," she said, then took the last of it off the stick as he watched. Her inhibitions nonexistent, she ran her tongue over her lips. "Cold, too. Wanna feel?"

He didn't say a word. Smiling, she leaned across the cushion and touched her lips to his just long enough to feel how warm his were—and how unresponsive. He didn't attempt to deepen the kiss.

She looked away. "I'm sorry. I don't know what got into me."

"Is there someone in your life who might not be too pleased that you're spending time alone with me, Mollie?"

"No." She couldn't just sit there. Embarrassment had probably turned her face as red as her lips. She took her Popsicle stick to the kitchen to throw away.

"No boyfriend?" he asked.

"Nope."

"So the heart-shaped box of candy in your refrigerator..."

"Left over from Valentine's Day."

Which was probably as much of an answer as he was going to get, Gray decided as she disappeared into the kitchen.

"Is there some woman who will challenge me to a duel for kissing you?" she called out.

"No." She called that a kiss? A press of cold lips that had lasted all of maybe two seconds? She'd caught him off guard—which was probably just as well, since a more personal relationship wasn't in his plans, which were getting hazier by the moment. The surge of protectiveness he felt toward her constantly surprised him, but the physical attraction amazed him. She was so young and innocent. And she had way too much faith in him.

If she only knew—

She came out of the kitchen. "Really, Gray? There's no special woman?"

"Most women don't like taking second place. My work consumes my time and energy."

"But you date. I've seen pictures." She frowned. "And not just Hollywood-type women. Samantha Simeon, right here in Minneapolis."

"I come out of my cyberworld long enough to date occasionally. As I'm sure you do."

She tucked her legs under her and rested her head against the sofa cushions. "I haven't been on a date since my mother died."

"You said that she passed away late last year."

"An aneurysm. There was no warning at all."

"My father died suddenly, too. I was eight."

"Oh!" She lifted her head. "Oh, I'm so sorry. At least I had my mom a lot longer. She was forty when she had me, but she'd never even looked middle-aged to me. We even shared clothes. I thought she was invincible. Sixty-one is too young to die."

"What about your father? You said he was gone before you were born."

She plucked at the upholstery fabric. "I never knew him."

Damn it. He couldn't read her. *Do you know that Stuart Fortune is your father, Mollie?* "Any other family?" he asked.

"None. How about you? Your mother remarried, obviously. Do you have siblings?"

He shook his head. "I guess we have a lot in common."

"Were you lonely as a child?"

Lonely was hardly the word. He'd been subjected to scandal, uprooted to California, given a new father and a new last name, commanded never to speak of his real father again. Ever. His life hadn't only been turned upside down but also inside out. "I was a loner," he said to Mollie.

"My mom was the best. It's been very hard without her."

She touched his hand that had clenched into a fist. "We've become morbid, haven't we? I think my head has settled down enough to take a computer lesson."

"It's probably a good night to learn how to use e-mail and maybe surf the Net a little."

"No one is going to believe this," she said a minute later as she sat in front of the computer. "I'm going to have to take pictures to prove you were here."

He dragged up a chair beside hers. "You can invite your friends over, if you want."

Mollie rejected the idea. Share him? No way. Not yet, anyway. Maybe not ever. He was her dream, after all. The reason for her sanity. She was afraid to diminish it by letting other people share in his attention. "Do you mind if we keep this relationship between us for a while?"

"Not at all. Show-and-tell was never my favorite part of the school day." He pointed to the Power key and told her to press it. "Do you know how to type?"

"I took two years of it in high school."

"Good. The rest is easy."

The sun set and the evening cooled. He taught. She practiced. He smiled at her contagious enthusiasm. She squeezed his arm when she found her flower shop listed in the on-line yellow pages. He was careful not to touch her, then a lock of hair fell over her shoulder and rested temptingly on her breast, rising and falling with her can't-sit-still excitement, but at the same time curtaining her face.

She stayed focused on the screen as she searched page after page of florists. After a few minutes he used just his fingertips to pull her hair back from her face. Softer than silk, he thought. He wondered what it would feel like against his chest—

Awareness sizzled through Mollie as his fingers grazed her shoulder blade. She turned toward him. His palm skimmed her arm. If his goal was to seduce her, he'd accomplished it. She tingled head to toe, partly from his touch, partly from his nearness, partly from the soapy scent that lingered on his skin, better than any spicy aftershave.

He pulled his hand back. Darn. She'd done something to ruin the mood. She lifted her brows in question.

"Your hair was in your face."

"Was it?" She tossed her head, feeling the familiar weight shift then settle against her back. His eyes darkened. He *was* attracted to her. But the women he usually dated were so different. So sophisticated.

She waited for him to say something, all the while feeling his body close to hers—not touching, but near enough to transfer heat. Conscious of how his gaze lowered to her mouth, she leaned toward him the slightest bit, willing to take advantage of the moment if he would only take the hint. Willing to test her theory that reality couldn't be as wonderful as her dreams. Her lips parted.

"This is a good place to stop for the night," he said, pushing his chair back and standing. "We can continue tomorrow, if you'd like."

She grabbed the papers stacked next to the computer and straightened them. "Um, sure. I'll provide dinner."

"I don't mind bringing it."

"You must be sick of restaurant food. I'm a decent cook, I promise."

"Okay. Good night, Mollie."

She grabbed his hand. "I need you—" she almost laughed at the panic in his eyes "—to show me how to shut down the computer." Could it be that he wasn't as sophisticated as she'd thought? That women scared him a little? The intriguing thought settled in her mind. Was that why his media interviews came across as all business? Because his confidence didn't extend to personal relationships?

No. He couldn't have risen to the position of CEO if he was socially inept.

So was it *her* that threw him off stride? The possibility that she might in any way intimidate him stunned her. Maybe no one had ever treated him like an ordinary human before. He'd been placed on a pedestal when he was twenty and his computer operating system debuted. Fame and fortune had soon followed.

Yet he seemed so alone...which was probably an illusion, or some wild imaginings on her part.

"You have to let go of my hand to turn off the program," he said quietly to her.

He talked her through the steps, writing them down so she could do it again without him.

When the hum of machinery stopped, she turned to him. "Thank you."

"Not as daunting as you thought, was it?"

"Not so far, but you're also a patient teacher. Wait'll we get to spreadsheets. I hate them even on paper. Math was always my least favorite subject."

"The worst that can happen is that you lose the information and have to reenter it. Be fearless."

Fearless. She would like to be fearless with him. She'd like to kiss him, really kiss him, to know how that spectacular body felt pressed against hers. She wasn't brave enough to make the first move, though, no matter how many *Cosmo* articles she'd read giving women permission to be the aggressors.

However, the man was either dense or not attracted, because he headed down the stairs. She followed to lock the door, but their good-nights were brief and cordial. She trekked back up the stairs.

Needing to unwind, Mollie relaxed in a bubble bath. Normally in bed by ten and up by six, she was still awake at midnight, like the night before. Finally she gave up, turned on the computer and waited for it to open.

The e-mail icon was lit. She stared at it for almost half a minute, trying to remember what to do. Finally she clicked on it. A new screen appeared, identifying mail awaiting her from GKMcGuire, the subject left blank. She clicked it open and read the message.

"I wanted to be your first. G."

Mollie felt her face heat. Her first e-mail, she assumed he meant. Either that or he *had* peeked into her birthday box before she hid it in her dresser.

She was trying to decide what to do when the mail icon flashed again.

From GKMcGuire: "I know you just got my message. Are you going to write me back? G."

How did he know? What trick was there to knowing that? And the most important question—how could she answer him? He'd told her how, but she hadn't practiced or written it down.

No sooner had she asked herself the question than the icon lit up.

From GKMcGuire: "Hit the Reply button, type in your message, then hit Send. G."

Mollie grinned, hit Reply, then typed: "Thank you for being so gentle. M." Send.

She waited. The icon flashed almost instantly.

From GKMcGuire: "Was it good for you? G."

She laughed as she clicked on Reply: "I'm still all aquiver. M." She waited a little longer for his next response.

From GKMcGuire: "I hope you remember me fondly. Good night. G."

From MollieS: "We never forget our first. Good night and thank you. M."

Gray shut down his computer, shutting down the temptation of her words at the same time. He had sunk to innuendo with her, displaying all the maturity of a teenager. Except that he hadn't done that even as a teenager. And she had responded in kind—

Irritated with himself, he slipped into bed, turned out the light and tucked his hands behind his head.

Knowing her past, he'd expected to find a bitter young woman. Mollie Shaw was anything but bitter. She'd accepted him into her life as if he belonged, had made him feel at home faster than anyone ever had, yet she didn't seem to want anything from him except a kiss—and that, he figured, was the wine doing the asking.

Her vulnerability reminded him of his life before Stuart Fortune had destroyed it. Memories of those carefree days surfaced too frequently now. He couldn't get those days back, but he could make up for the loss. And he could get Mollie the fiscal base she needed.

Muttering a curse, he switched on the light, tossed the sheet aside and crossed the room to where he'd draped his jeans over a chair. He dug into a pocket, coming up with a Popsicle stick, stained red, like her lips had been. Red and cold.

He returned to bed, jammed pillows behind his back and turned the stick over and over in his hands. He could barely remember snatching it out of her trash can when he'd tossed the empty wine bottle away. He'd acted on a whim, as she had when she'd kissed him.

That memory drifted in. Red and cold. And cherry sweet. Her cheeks had flushed afterward.

In his experience, kissing led to sex. Given their potential partnership, he couldn't sleep with Mollie, therefore he couldn't kiss her. It was that simple—unlike the woman herself, who was becoming more and more complicated.

He tapped the stick to his mouth, then tossed it on the nightstand, annoyed. Obsession was beyond his experience. It had been a long time since he'd wanted something he couldn't have.

But she made him laugh. And she comforted without knowing it. Even better, she was as fiery as her red hair. In bed, too? he wondered.

And what would she say if she knew he was wondering about that?

Four

———

"**N**ever?" Mollie gaped at the back of Gray's head as she stood behind him the next evening. She'd closed her shop promptly at 6:00 p.m., then hurried upstairs. He'd spent the afternoon entering her previous year's wholesale orders into a "tracking program," as he called it. "Gray McGuire, you have never in your life been on a picnic?"

"Not that I can recall."

He was seated at the computer, watching the printer as it cranked out sheet after sheet of graphs and charts. She looked over his shoulder at the monitor, where a colorful pie chart filled the screen.

"Maybe when I was too young to remember," he added.

"That is un-American. Not even on the Fourth of July?"

"Not even."

"We are filling that gap in your life experience tonight."

"Okay." He snagged the stack of papers from the printer. "Take a look at these. As soon as I feed in the actual sales information, you'll know exactly where your potential for loss is. See here—"

Leaning around him, she reached for the papers just as he tipped his head back to say something. His head bumped against her sternum, right between her breasts. She didn't move. Neither did he.

She matched her breathing to his, a rhythm that teased her with awareness of him as a man, a partner, a mate. She loved the weight of his head resting, almost nestling, between her breasts, making them swell and ache. Her nipples pressed into her bra. Down low, she felt her pulse pound.

Gray turned his head slightly, enough to feel the softness of her breast against his ear.

She stepped back, but the spell wasn't broken for him. Need froze him in place.

"We won't talk business until after dinner, okay? I'm going to change clothes, then fix our picnic. We'll walk down to the park." Her voice faded as she moved away.

Her scent lingered. He wished he could pin it down, but it changed with her mood, her body temperature.

"I went to the grocery store before I opened up the shop," she called out, jarring him out of his musings. "My refrigerator is overflowing with choices."

"I brought wine," he said. He typed a few keystrokes, sending the chart off the screen and bringing up a graph in its place. He waited until he heard her bedroom door shut before he took his hands off the keyboard. The back of his head still burned from the feel of her. Bells and whistles rang in his head, warning him of an impending crash of his logic system.

He checked his e-mail one last time. Another message from his stepfather, wondering when Gray would be resuming his responsibilities in California. The censure stung. He'd assumed his responsibilities early and well, had rarely taken a day off since he'd developed the computer operating system that had helped to revolutionize the fledgling home-computer industry.

Since then—a never-ending cycle of software to create, upgrades to design and the company to run since his stepfather had relinquished control to Gray years ago. The single-source business had mushroomed into a conglomerate under Gray's risky push for growth. Some might even call it an empire. He was grateful his stepfather had never figured out that Gray had taken such huge risks because he hadn't created the company, therefore had nothing to lose.

He looked away from the screen, seeing nothing. He'd referred to James McGuire as his father since his mother's marriage to the man almost twenty-five years ago. Had been ordered to, as if his real father had never walked the earth. His mother would not be pleased that Gray was thinking of James McGuire as his *step*father.

His mother, however, would not be pleased about a lot of things, particularly not Gray's plans for justice. The past wasn't only dead and buried to her, it didn't exist. Life hadn't begun for her until the day she'd become Mrs. James McGuire.

Life had yet to begin for Gray.

He shut down the computer without replying to the e-mail. It was Friday night. Date night. And Gray intended to enjoy it.

"Just because I haven't been on a picnic doesn't mean I don't know how it works," Gray said as he helped Mollie spread out a blanket that had probably been dragged along on a hundred picnics, given the tattered softness of the fabric. The evening was perfect, warm enough that Mollie wore shorts, and breezy enough to mold her blouse to her breasts.

"You eat fried chicken," he continued, "potato salad and pickles, then watermelon for dessert. And you spit the seeds on the ground. Then you lie back on the blanket and groan about how much food you ate while you watch the fireworks."

"You helped me pack the basket, so you know you got the food all wrong. And if you spit watermelon seeds on the ground, they sprout. It's annoying."

"But fireworks," he said. "There have to be fireworks."

"If you want 'em, you'll have to provide 'em."

She bent to straighten a corner of the blanket, her legs pale and smooth, her rear an appealing focal point. Fireworks, indeed, but in the form of one Mollie Shaw, human sparkler.

They created sandwiches of fresh bakery bread, smoked turkey, two kinds of cheeses and a dark, tangy mustard. Other containers yielded pasta salad, fresh and marinated vegetables, and watermelon, already cut into bite-size pieces. Then rich, chocolaty brownies, so moist and gooey they had to lick the chocolate off their fingers. And the California white zinfandel wine they drank managed to complement all the different flavors.

Mollie lay flat on her back. "I'm so full," she groaned. She'd nursed one glass of wine throughout the meal, having no intention of being tipsy again. He probably already thought she was too young for him, if his indulgent smile was any indication. Of some consolation was the fact he seemed to be losing some of his seriousness. Neither of them spoke of their e-mail exchange the night before, when they'd written things to each other that they never would have said aloud. She wished she'd known how to print them off and save them.

She glanced toward Gray as he rested his back against a tree and watched some children play nearby, hollering and laughing, bringing a smile to his face. She wondered how rare it was for him to relax. He took a sip of wine, then stretched his arm across his upraised knee, letting the half-full wineglass dangle from his fingers. His eyes closed.

Mollie closed hers, as well, feeling the warm evening drift over her.

"You're easy to be with," he said after a while.

She stirred, rolling to her side and propping her head on her hand. His words answered a question she'd been pondering— why did a man with his many responsibilities have so much time to spend with her? Answer? Because she didn't demand anything from him.

"I suppose people always want something from you."

"Pretty much."

"Ever thought about changing your life?"

It took him a few seconds to answer. "Now and then."

"What brings you to the Twin Cities?"

"I'm considering acquiring a company here."

"Acquiring, as in buying it? Or taking over?" She regretted asking the questions, because he lost his contented look.

"Whatever works."

"Yet you have time to teach me computers."

"Not a hardship, I assure you," he said. He slid down to

stretch out beside her, facing her. "You're the best kind of student."

"What kind is that?"

"Balky."

"Me? Why, Mr. McGuire, I'm the easiest-going woman you'd ever hope to meet."

"Balky," he repeated, matter of fact.

"Well, you're pushy."

"Only when I know I'm right." He refilled her wineglass, then looked at her. "I'm going home tomorrow."

Her heart skipped. "Will you be back?"

He nodded. "In the meantime—"

"I know. We'll e-mail." She wondered if he had hair on his chest. She wondered what he would do if she pressed her mouth to that tempting vee of tanned flesh revealed by his open collar.

"I may even call you," he said.

"Be still my heart." She thumped her fist between her breasts, watching his gaze drop, then linger, even after she let her arm rest on the blanket again. Her body tingled as much as it had in her apartment. And all he'd done was look.

A tiny leaf swirled down, landing on his head. She resisted the temptation to brush it away, because she liked how it looked against his hair—and because he didn't seem comfortable being touched. Touch was one of the things she missed most these days. She and her mother had hugged every day. Every single day.

"We should probably get back to your place and start working," he said, sitting up.

Gray had just put the first container into the cooler when he sensed her inching toward him. She lifted her hand. He went still. Her fingers brushed his hair, then she held a small leaf for him to see.

"It landed on you a while ago."

His reaction was ridiculous—getting aroused by a touch so faint it was hardly worth calling it that. A whisper of contact, no more.

"Thanks," he murmured, tossing the rest of their stuff into the cooler, then jamming it shut.

"My mom and I used to picnic here a lot," she said, a catch in her voice. "I've been back since, but this is the first real picnic."

He looked at her. She gazed into the distance.

"At times like this, I miss her so much I can hardly breathe."

He clenched his teeth until his jaw hurt. "I thought I'd never get over my father's death," he said, the memories slamming into him. He hadn't talked about his father in so long. So very long. "Nothing ever replaced him."

"No. Nothing could. But maybe having a family of your own would help?"

He hesitated. That was her dream, not his. Family life hadn't amounted to much. But he appeased Mollie, anyway. "Maybe," he said.

"I want a family of my own so much I can taste it."

Her words didn't surprise him, but brought anger instead. She had a family, one that had ignored her all these years. She should have had their support, their love.

The list of crimes against Stuart Fortune grew longer.

"One last thing to show you," Gray said three hours later. He closed the screen, then opened another. "Here's your dictionary."

"I think it would be easier to use the real thing," she said. "It's two feet away."

"Not if you're already on-line. Here. Let's look up something." He typed the word *leprechaun.* "'One of a race of elves in Irish folklore who can reveal hidden treasure to someone who catches him,'" he read. "One who screeches," he added with a smile at Mollie.

"Yarg doesn't screech, he shrieks. There's a difference, you know."

"Yarg. What kind of name is that, anyway?"

She didn't answer right away. He took his gaze off the screen and saw her face pinken.

"Celtic," she said, her voice strange.

"Do you want to look it up?"

"No!" She laughed a little. "I mean, I've had about as many

lessons as I can take in one night." She straightened the papers beside the computer. "Do you still think I'm the best kind of student?"

"Sure. Why?"

"You have more patience than anyone I've ever known."

"Did you expect to be an expert after only a few hours?"

"I hate the learning process," she grumbled. "I feel stupid."

"Which you aren't. And it's been valuable for me, teaching you. I can see where we need to clarify the instructions in the manual for the novice user. The jargon slows you down, yet ours is supposed to be the most user-friendly system on the market." He stood and stretched. He had to leave now, before sitting so close to her made him do something he would regret— like kiss her. It was bad enough he'd spent the past few hours adrift in her fragrance and distracted by the appealing frown of concentration on her face, the memory of her touch washing over him like gentle waves.

"Be fearless, Mollie. I've saved everything to floppy disks, so even if you mess something up, you won't lose it entirely. The problem is that until you get a second phone line, I can't talk you through anything."

Her gaze was leveled directly at his mouth.

"Did you hear me?" he asked.

Visibly startled, she raised her eyes to his, then she stood. "I'll be fearless. And I'll master this by the time you come back. When do you think that might be?"

"It depends on how much has piled up at home and how quickly things transpire with the business here." He extended his hand to her. "Goodbye for now."

She hesitated, slipped her hand into his, then didn't let go. "This is a lot to ask," she said quietly, "but I would really like to hug you goodbye. I know we have a business relationship, but I feel so close to you tonight. Our talk about my mother and your father and—"

He pulled her against him, wrapping his arms around her, feeling her arms come around his back and hold tight. She burrowed closer, pressing her face into his neck so that he could feel her breath, warm and unsteady against his skin.

"Don't let go," she whispered.

He didn't move his hands, although he wanted to soothe and comfort. To explore and arouse. To satisfy. Himself and her. Would she disappear if he did? Fly away on fairy wings?

She murmured his name. He heard the emotion behind it, the need that mirrored his. But there was too much at stake to respond to her needs or his own. The risks were high enough without adding to them.

"I'll be in touch," he said, pushing away from her, not looking back as he hurried down the stairs, then to the front door.

He turned the dead bolt, twisted the doorknob and pulled.

"Thanks for everything," she said from behind him. She'd followed like a comet's tail—undoubtedly to lock up after he left.

Nothing in his life had prepared him for Mollie Shaw.

He'd never known anyone like her, and probably never would again. He could barely remember being as trusting as she, as vulnerable. Yet once upon a time, he had been. The memory of that innocence made him hesitate now.

He started to turn. His foot bumped against something— The screeching leprechaun, silent now, his switch turned off, but oddly a reminder of his responsibilities to the young woman who waited, quiet and patient. The woman who surrounded herself with elves and fairies and other bits of magic. She'd known love. In that she was richer than he.

The glow of a streetlamp illuminated her face. She smiled, the warmth filling her eyes. Again came the fleeting feeling she might fade away.

"You're a hard woman to resist," he said, sliding his hands in his pockets.

A few beats passed before she responded. "I hope you're not waiting for an apology. That would be a logical expectation, of course, but logic is only one component of my database."

The spell was broken. "I love it when you talk techno," he said.

Mollie laughed. She cupped his arm, letting her thumb slide under his shirtsleeve to caress his skin, the muscles bunching beneath. She wondered why he felt he had to resist her, but she didn't ask. For now, it was enough that the attraction was mutual. "Have a safe flight home, Gray."

He nodded, then he was gone.

She lingered at the front window until he drove out of sight, then she danced up the stairs and pirouetted into the bathroom to run a bath. She couldn't stop smiling. She, Mollie Shaw of Minneapolis, Minnesota, was a hard woman to resist! Mollie laughed at the idea. While soaking in the tub, however, she considered his words a little more seriously.

What had she learned about him? What could make it hard for him to resist her?

Hmm. He seemed to be much more of a loner than she would have thought, given his important job and his worldwide recognition. Maybe *because* of it? Definitely a possibility.

What else? People generally wanted something from him, he'd admitted. But he found her easy to be with.

She would like to see him in action, in his own environment, so that she could compare him to the man she was coming to know and care about, beyond the surface of photos and news articles. He could spend three hours never crossing the line between teacher and student, then with one simple sentence, send her impression of him spinning. "You're a hard woman to resist." Those words clung to her heart. They would for a long time.

After climbing out of the tub she dressed in a cool summer nightie, then folded back her bedding and slid under the sheet. A few seconds later she plopped herself in front of the computer. Maybe he'd sent her an e-mail.

No mail.

Disappointment made her shoulders droop. She wondered how pushy she should be with him, given that he liked that she *didn't* push him. On the other hand, she didn't want to be passive in this relationship, either.

Relationship. The word swirled, settled. She pressed her shoulders back and set her fingertips on the keyboard.

From MollieS: "I'll miss you. Hurry back. M." She hit the Send key, then swallowed her panic at what she'd done.

He responded in a flash. From GKMcGuire: "Come with me."

Mollie straightened in her chair and read the words several times. Her fingers shook. From MollieS: "Why?"

From GKMcGuire: "You should meet my parents, so that you can get an idea of what kind of party to plan."

From MollieS: "I have to work."

From GKMcGuire: "You don't work seven days a week."

She glanced at the telephone. Something this important needed to be discussed, not electronically communicated. And yet he seemed to open up with her more in this forum.

From MollieS: "I do the altar flowers for three churches on Sunday morning. The store reopens on Tuesday morning at 10:00, but I have to be here by 8:00 for a delivery."

From GKMcGuire: "Which is plenty of time. Say yes. I'll cancel my flight for tomorrow and have the company jet sent to pick us up on Sunday morning, at whatever time you can make it. You'll be back in time on Tuesday."

Tiresomely sensible. The label she'd given herself echoed in her head. She wanted adventure, and Gray was offering it. A trip to California. The chance to meet his family.

The chance to spend a lot of time alone with him. On a private jet. No other passengers or flight attendants or anyone. Just them. For hours. Could he resist her for that long?

From MollieS: "Okay." She hit Send, then covered her face with her hands. What had she done? She didn't have the right clothes to wear. She couldn't afford new ones, even if she had time to shop. She was going to meet his *parents.*

From GKMcGuire: "Great. We can't tell them you're the party planner, because I think I'm going to keep it a surprise."

From MollieS: "So, who am I?"

From GKMcGuire: "My lover?"

From MollieS: "Right. I'm sure your mother will take one look at me and decide to be worried I was tainting her baby boy."

Gray tried to picture his mother's reaction. Actually, Mollie was exactly the kind of woman his mother would worry about. He hadn't brought many women home, but the ones he had fit nicely into the McGuire expectation of sophistication and status. Mollie broke that mold with a clean karate chop down the middle.

From GKMcGuire: "I don't live with my parents, but we'll stay with them since the time is limited. They will make assumptions, but they won't expect us to sleep in the same room. Can you manage that small lie comfortably? Naturally at the party we'll clue them in on your role."

From MollieS: "If you honestly believe they'll think I'm your girlfriend, I'll be happy to play my part."

From GKMcGuire: "Then it's settled. I'll drop by the shop tomorrow and we'll discuss details. I don't want you to worry. You'll fit in better than you think. G."

He stayed on-line several minutes, in case she had something else to ask, but she didn't. She was probably standing at her open closet, stewing about what to wear. If he thought she would accept the gift, he would take her shopping after work, but he understood and admired her pride. He wouldn't put her on the spot by offering.

In the meantime he had to cancel a flight, order the company jet and invite himself and Mollie to stay with his parents, not trusting himself to take her to his apartment. The first two could be handled by computer. The third could, as well, but he picked up the phone instead, glancing at the clock, determining it was 9:30 p.m. in California.

"Good evening, Endicott," Gray said when the butler answered phone. "Is my mother at home?"

"Of course, Mr. McGuire. Please hold."

"Hello, darling. What a nice surprise." Gretchen McGuire's voice never varied in pitch. Happy or distressed, she sounded velvety smooth. "Have you come home?"

He touched a red-stained Popsicle stick to his mouth. *Home.* He wondered where that was, exactly.

Five

Mollie glanced over her shoulder at the three women who were "Just looking, thank you" a little after noon the next day. She was exhausted and energized at the same time, having stayed up until almost 2:00 a.m. sorting through her clothes, trying to come up with a few outfits to wear on the trip. If she could get to the mall right after work, she could pick up a new pair of sandals, plus an off-white cotton blazer that would dress up anything.

"Oh, how darling!" one woman exclaimed, lifting down a vine basket Mollie had decorated with dried roses and straw-flowers on the outside instead of the inside. A wire-trimmed ribbon the color of the roses brightened the whole package. She'd come up with the idea last month and had sold twenty of them, each a little different from the next.

Gray had won one at the ball, she remembered. He'd found her because of it.

The woman set the basket on the counter in front of Mollie. "I'd like three more of these, two with yellow roses, if you can."

"How soon do you need them?" Mollie asked. "I've got pink roses on hand, but I'll have to order the yellow."

"For next weekend. Is that possible?"

"No problem. I can have them ready Friday morning. Would you like them exactly alike in style or should I be creative?"

"Oh, can you individualize them? I didn't realize you made them yourself."

Mollie assured her she did, then she wrote down the order before ringing up the one basket for her to take. As she and her friends went out the door, Kelly Sinclair Fortune came in, her five-month-old daughter, Annie, squirming and giggling in her arms.

"Here's my sweet baby girl," Mollie cooed as she reached for the smiling, drooling infant, a blue-eyed blonde just like her mom. "You actually left your honeymoon haven to come see me, Kel?"

"Can't eat dessert all day," Kelly said, "no matter how scrumptious it is."

"Your steady consumption of *dessert,* as you call it, must be nonfat. You're down to prebaby form. Obviously, you're loving married life."

"*Loving* is such a mild word for what I feel, Mol. You've just got to try it for yourself." She handed the baby a teething ring. "She's going to drool all over you."

Marriage did agree with Kelly, Mollie decided, never having seen her so radiant. Five years older than Mollie, Kelly had been first her baby-sitter and then her friend, a relationship cemented by the commonalities of having single mothers and growing up in the same neighborhood.

"I fully intend to try marriage someday," Mollie said, coming nose to nose with Annie, who dropped the teething ring to tug Mollie's hair into her mouth. "And having a few of these little precious gems."

"She's a wonder." Kelly plunked the diaper bag on the counter, then scooped up the teething ring. "So, what's happening with you? You never call. You haven't once accepted my invitation for Sunday dinner with Mac and Annie and me. I'm worried about you."

"I'm fine. Honestly, I am. Doing better every day. Business is picking up so much that I'm going to hire an assistant."

"You've met a man."

Startled speechless, Mollie stared at her friend.

"A, you're considering hiring someone—which means you want some time off now and then. B, you're glowing."

Mollie felt her cheeks flush, much as they had been for the past few days just being around Gray. But she couldn't tell Kelly about Gray, because she would tell Mac, and he might mention it to someone else in the Fortune family. And Mollie wasn't ready to share Gray with them yet.

Actually, what she wanted to do was to take out a full-page ad in the *StarTribune,* run an announcement on every TV channel and maybe even hire a plane to tow a banner: Gray McGuire asked Mollie Shaw to be his girlfriend.

Okay, so it was only a pretend girlfriend. But his mother was going to assume they were lovers—

Kelly waved a hand in front of Mollie's face. "Cripes. He must be something."

Annie stuck her fingers in Mollie's mouth, saving her from answering.

"What's his name? What does he look like? He'd better treat you well."

"Slow down. You don't have to be big sister, okay? I'm not ready to introduce him to you because he might think I have plans for him, and it hasn't reached that point. You'll meet him as soon as I think it won't scare him off."

"You always could keep a secret."

"You used to say that like it was a compliment, Kel."

Kelly grinned. She lifted Annie into her arms as the door opened and an elderly couple came in. Mollie greeted them by name, then headed to the refrigerator case to get the small bouquet she fixed weekly for them to take to their daughter's grave.

As soon as they left, Kelly looked at Mollie as if she wasn't going to take no for an answer—no matter what the question was. "We came to invite you to dinner tomorrow. Mac will be there, of course, plus Chloe and Mason." She cocked her head. "Speaking of Chloe and Mason—do they seem all right to you? Are the wedding plans still full speed ahead?"

"I haven't spoken to them in a couple of weeks. Do you think something's wrong?"

"Nothing I can put my finger on." She tugged her hair out of her daughter's fist. "So, how about dinner?"

"I've got plans for tomorrow."

"With the mystery man?"

"Yes. And that's all I'm going to tell you."

The front door opened.

"Top of the mornin' to ye!" Yarg shrieked.

"I'm going to decommission you," Gray threatened placidly as he walked by the plastic creature, who winked as if on cue.

Mollie waited to see if Kelly and Gray acknowledged each other, hoping not. Kelly hadn't attended the charity ball, so there was a chance she didn't know who he was. When neither showed any sign of recognition, Mollie looked meaningfully at Gray. "I'll be right with you, sir."

Sir? Gray glanced at the blond woman holding the baby. "I'm in no hurry," he said in return, catching the flicker of gratitude in Mollie's eyes before he moved to examine the items she'd chosen to display in her new hutch.

"Well, we want to get home to Daddy, don't we, sweetheart?" the woman said to the baby as she grabbed a canvas bag, then leaned across the counter toward Mollie and lowered her voice a little. "I want all the details, and soon. Promise you'll call or I'm gonna sic Mac on you. And you know Mac can pull answers out of anyone."

Mac Fortune? Gray wondered. Mac was the oldest son of Stuart Fortune's brother, Emmet. Mac's wedding had netted Mollie her first job as a wedding planner, which had led to the upcoming nuptials of Chloe Fortune and Mason Chandler, the fairy-tale-princess event yet to come.

After the woman left, Mollie came around the counter and thanked him.

"Friend of yours?" he asked.

"Kelly Fortune. We grew up together. I was afraid you'd met already."

"Afraid?"

"I'm not ready to share you with my friends yet."

There was nothing coy in her expression, just the truth of her words, which he respected and was glad of, even as he also wondered why she wanted to keep him a secret.

"I've probably become too independent since Mom died, but

I don't want to lean on anyone. My friends mean well, but they tend to offer advice freely."

"You told me you always listen to advice."

Her cheeks pinkened. "Yours was relevant to my business, and you have the qualifications to do so."

"Do you think your friends would advise you against this trip?"

Her eyes danced merrily. "Hmm. I'm only guessing, of course, but I think they just might try to talk me out of flying to California with a handsome, sexy man I met only three days ago. A man who, according to the tabloids, dates a new woman every week. Stunning blondes, exotic brunettes—"

"Beautiful redheads?"

"I'm not beautiful," she said quietly, seriously, her eyes searching his.

"I'm apparently an expert in the matter."

"You're just being kind."

Kind—a word he hadn't heard before in reference to himself. The descriptions usually involved words like *grim* and *focused. Solitary. Distant.* No one had called him handsome or sexy until just a minute ago. He didn't have any illusions. Money and status were powerful draws for most people. "I'm not being kind, Mollie."

She clasped her hands together. "It doesn't even matter, does it? We're doing business together, right?"

He hesitated only an instant. "Right. What time do you think we can leave tomorrow?"

"Six-thirty."

"In the morning?"

She grinned. "I asked Tony to deliver the baskets, so all I have to do is put the arrangements together."

"Which means you'll want to get to bed early."

"You think I'm going to be able to sleep? I've never flown before. I'll be way too excited to sleep. But I do need to go shopping right after work and pick up a couple of things for the trip."

"Do you mind if I tag along?"

"I don't mind. As long as you don't try to buy me anything."

"Not even dinner?"

"Oh. Well. Dinner. That'd be okay."

"You don't have to worry about dressing up for my parents, Mollie."

She crossed her arms. "That's such a male reaction."

"In case you hadn't noticed—"

"You're a man." She fluttered her eyelashes at him. "Oh, I noticed."

He didn't know how to respond to a flirtatious Mollie, so he pulled a floppy disk out of his pocket and held it up. "I've brought another program to install on your computer."

"Like I don't have enough to learn already?"

"This one will do your taxes for you."

"Really? Are you going to install it now?"

"I thought I would. Is that a problem?"

"Um. You kind of need to ignore the condition of my apartment. It kind of looks like a tornado swept through."

Gray doubted that. Her shop and apartment were like well-tended gardens and just as colorful. Not to mention home to a legendary leprechaun.

He told her he'd see her later, then he climbed the stairs. A tidy living room greeted him. He kept walking, needing to see what she considered messy. The kitchen sparkled. The bathroom still smelled like a bouquet—and her. He breathed in the scent for a minute—still unable to identify it—then he moved on to the bedroom.

Chaos. Clothes strewn on both twin beds—hers wasn't even made. Drawers pulled open, with feminine…*stuff* spilling out. He absorbed the dazzling and colorful sight. His experience with the opposite sex had never resulted in his living with one. He found the scene endearing. She was more nervous than he'd thought. Perhaps he should reconsider throwing her into the lions' den so soon. His parents could be formidable with people of their own kind. With an innocent like Mollie…

The thought faded. He didn't want to look too closely at his motivations for subjecting her to his parents. They would be courteous, if a little intimidating, but he expected to keep her within his protection throughout the short trip—

The concept of his being her knight in shining armor startled him. *Knight.* The word jarred him. This wasn't a game of Dungeons and Dragons. It was someone's life. An innocent someone's life. If she knew his intentions—

The words had begun to haunt him. He was too used to making a plan and following through without a second thought. And his intent to bury Stuart Fortune—to ruin him—hadn't kept him from a peaceful sleep, not for a minute.

His conscience was clear. This was payback, plain and simple. And Mollie's gains would more than balance any temporary embarrassment or hurt. He would see to that.

As he turned to go back into the living room, a bit of sparkle caught his eye—the glittery box with the birthday cake and candles on it...open.

"Is that all you're getting?" Gray asked as Mollie headed for the store exit hours later, her stride determined. "Sandals and a jacket?"

"That's all I came for."

He'd watched her gaze linger on a few other items—a long, flower-printed dress in shades of green, a jade necklace, a pin that looked like the fairy on her counter bell. He'd been assaulted by an unreasonable urge to see her try on the things she liked, to see her eyes light up as she modeled them for him. Instead he'd pushed that fantasy aside at the same time that he shoved his fists in his pockets.

He had entered her financial data into her computer. He knew exactly how much money she made. Not enough for luxuries. *Soon, though, Mollie. Soon.*

"I suppose you make a list to take to the grocery store, too, so that you avoid impulse shopping," he said, holding open the door.

She glanced over her shoulder at him. "Don't you? You seem like a *list* kind of person."

"I don't shop."

"Never?"

"I don't grocery shop," he clarified as they walked toward his car. "I lease the penthouse of a hotel in the Silicon Valley near my office. I've never used my kitchen except for cleaning up after eating takeout."

He couldn't decipher her expression. "What?" he asked.

"If I'd tried to imagine how you lived, I never would've come close. I figured you would have a mansion or something, with everything operated electronically by some lights-flashing, computer-brain nerve center. A few servants, maybe. Gardeners. You know, a life *style,* not just a life.''

"What would one person do with all that? The hotel takes care of the cleaning. I eat out most of the time or order room service. And except for a computer in my home office, I avoid computerizing anything. It's too consuming.''

"Meaning, you like the simple life?'' she asked as he unlocked the car.

"Well, my definition of simple may differ from yours. Or from anyone else's, for that matter. But complications frustrate me. It's enough running the company while still designing software. This week has been like a vacation, even though I've also worked.'' He shut her door, then walked around the car and climbed in.

"If I didn't like my job, I would quit.''

Gray slid the key into the ignition and started the engine. "It's not that simple for me.''

"But it's not impossible?''

Mollie waited as he considered the question. He seemed to forget the car was running. He seemed to forget *her.* After a minute she touched his arm. He jerked back, startling her.

"You left the planet. Is this how you get when you think hard about something?''

He backed the car out of the parking space. "If you're looking for someone to pay attention to you all the time, I'm not your man.''

Cool words and an icy tone, as if he'd been accused all his life of not paying attention. Had he been? A nonconformist forced to conform?

"Actually, I admire the way you can concentrate like that. I'm always thinking about five things at once.'' She watched him relax. "Which is why you'll probably get totally exasperated teaching me the computer.''

"I haven't yet.''

"Give it time.'' She grinned at him. "I know myself. I have a short attention span.''

"You've done great, Mollie.''

Because you're the one teaching me. Heck, if he'd wanted to teach her how to scuba dive, she would have followed him, mask, flippers and tank into Lake Superior, even though she could barely swim, even though the dark, icy waters of the lake terrified her.

"What are you smiling about?" he asked.

"I don't know what cosmic phenomenon brought you into my life right now, but I'm grateful for it. I've been sad for too long. My mother wouldn't have liked that." She leaned across the console and kissed his cheek, wished she could snuggle against him. She needed him. Couldn't he see that? "Thank you."

"I wish I'd met her."

"She was really something. She'd been married to a man who abused her. It took a lot for her to escape that life and start over. She had proof of him beating her, so he didn't fight the divorce. I don't think he ever learned where she moved. Their divorce was final right before I was born, and she took back her maiden name."

"I see where you get your strength."

"She had plenty of it. I'm really proud of what she did with her life after that. It was an uphill battle for a long time, though, especially with a baby to provide for all by herself. We were closer than some mothers and daughters, probably, because of what she'd gone through."

He glanced in her direction. "Are you wary of men because of it?"

"Not at all. One bad apple, you know."

"She never remarried?"

"No. But she had men friends, relationships that lasted for years, even. And it was a little difficult finding single, compatible men at her age."

"Yes, I imagine it would be." Gray had his answer. Mollie believed her mother's ex-husband was her father. Why hadn't her mother told her the truth? Karen had been compensated well—

He gripped the steering wheel. Stuart had paid her off. Bought her silence. And Karen Shaw had been an honorable woman who'd kept her end of the bargain, while Stuart had gotten off scot-free.

Mollie watched Gray's expression close up. She hoped she hadn't caused it. "I'm a little worried about what's going to happen tomorrow," she said. "Do you think your parents will believe we're having an—a...relationship?"

"Why not?"

"Don't lovers—" she struggled getting that enormous word out "—act, I don't know, loverlike?"

"Not in front of my parents."

"Oh." Disappointment surged through her. She wanted to show him what he was missing, keeping his distance. "You mean, it's okay to *be* lovers, but we can't *act* like we are?"

"Exactly. Displays of affection are reserved for moments of extreme privacy."

Darn. She'd hoped to get in a little practice with him before they left tomorrow, so they would look right together.

Comfortable with each other. Practice makes perfect—

"Just be yourself," he said as he parked in front of her shop. "No one can resist that."

His offhanded compliments were treasured gifts. He'd told her she was beautiful—she could add a star to her nineteenth-birthday candle because of that. She was a hard woman to resist, he'd said. Then there were the other gifts he gave without knowing it—her tenth-birthday wish, when she'd wished to take a trip—*anywhere!*—would come true this weekend.

She turned toward him. "Thank you for dinner and for taking me shopping."

"My pleasure. Do you really think you'll be ready by six-thirty?"

"That's what time Tony will come by. If I shower afterward instead of before, I would need another half hour."

"All right. Why don't I pick you up at seven, and we can stop for breakfast before we head to the airport. We'll lose two hours going west. I don't want to get there too early in the morning."

Mollie lifted her bag from the floorboard and into her arms. She set her hand on the door handle, but hesitated. "I don't think you know just how big of an adventure this is for me, Gray. I can't thank you enough."

Gray resisted the how-about-a-good-night-kiss expression in her eyes. Anticipation played with his imagination as he visualized such a kiss. Warmth rushed through his veins, pooled low, then simmered. Attraction hadn't been part of the plan, but he couldn't deny it, either. Her wide mouth looked eminently kissable, her sleek body exceptionally touchable. Only that huge Off-Limits sign that was lit in neon above her head stopped him from acting on his desire. He was supposed to avenge her, protect her—not seduce her.

"Don't stay up all night fretting, Mollie," he said. "Everything will be fine."

"You're not coming up?"

He shook his head. "I need to finish a project."

"I'll see you in the morning, then."

Gray waited until she was safely inside her shop, then drove to a small, tidy house on a tree-lined street not far from hers. After grabbing an envelope from the glove compartment, he approached the structure with a resolute stride.

"Mr. McGuire," the silver-haired man who opened the door said, a curious emphasis on the name.

"Mr. Swensen. May I come in?"

Gunnar Swensen shut the door behind Gray but didn't invite him farther into the house. "You've come to a decision?" the man asked.

Gray passed him the envelope. "Everything checked out."

The man withdrew the bank book from the envelope, then examined the amount written there. "This is more than we discussed."

"Yes."

He stared at Gray for a minute, his eyes cautious and weary. "What if you decide to do nothing?"

"That won't happen."

"If you are in an accident or become ill suddenly and die—"

"The money is still yours," Gray interrupted, hearing the strain in his own voice. He headed for the door.

"You are nothing like your father," Gunnar said.

Gray didn't suffer from any illusions. He knew he wasn't universally loved, as his father had been. Respect was the most he could hope for. Still, the knife-sharp words sliced Gray's heart neatly in two for the second time in his life. "Lucky for you," he said to the man just before the door shut. He'd needed proof of Mollie's parentage. Now he had it, hoarded by Gunnar Swensen all these years.

The unsettling business behind him, he drove out of the city and into the countryside trying to bury the memories surfacing like a meteor shower. In his mind he struggled once again to stuff them back into the dark place they lived.

When that task was done, he returned to his hotel, booted his computer, then scanned the list of mail awaiting him. He ignored it all except the one from MollieS: "We can't even hold hands in front of your parents?"

He stared at the screen. A smile pulled at his mouth. Mollie, Mollie, Mollie. Picturing her earnest expression, he laughed. But the laughter soon faded, as did the smile. When the truth came out, would she be as irreversibly changed as he had been?

The phone rang. A few minutes later he hung up, satisfied. Knight Star Systems had lost out in the bidding for a deal that would have been the biggest in their history, a bid they should have been awarded easily.

Stuart should be fitting the final pieces of the puzzle together. Questioning his abilities. Anguishing over having to lay off employees. His character was about to be tested—failure tested a man.

Soon, everyone would know Stuart Fortune wasn't perfect. *Tick-tock, Stuart. Tick...tock.*

Six

Mollie wondered if she was going to survive the roller coaster of a day—the exhilaration of her first plane flight followed by the stomach-plummeting anticipation of meeting Gray's parents, which was imminent. They had just turned off the main road into a long, imposing driveway, bordered by flower beds and trees and shrubbery.

"Be fearless."

She smiled at Gray's quiet words, wishing he would kiss her for luck. She couldn't figure out what he was waiting for.

"And be yourself," he added.

"You wouldn't know it to look at me now," she said after blowing out a breath, "but I actually do enjoy meeting new people. It's just that your parents aren't people."

He laughed.

"You know what I mean." Her cheeks heated. Great. Just in time to meet his mother. "If I were coming here on business, as their party planner, I would know how to act. I would have a list of questions. But since I'm pretending to be your girlfriend, or whatever you would call it, I'm working without a safety net.''

''My mother will discuss the weather and her garden, and perhaps her charity work. She won't ask questions that are too personal, in case the answers might be unpleasant. She will be shocked that you live in Minneapolis, but you won't know it from her expression, which won't change.''

''This all sounds so encouraging.'' She could see the house now. Mansion. Whatever the old, beautiful, formal structure was called with its massive columns and interesting facades. ''What about your father?''

''He won't have much to say. He'll probably take me off to his office to bring me up to speed on what happened while I was gone. His position is chairman of the board, by the way. McGuire Enterprises is his creation, although it's changed tremendously through the years. He started it before he married my mother.''

''And now you run it.''

''Right.'' Gray parked in front of the house. ''Here we are.''

The house looked bigger and grander from up close. *No turning back.*

''Our luggage will be taken to our rooms,'' he said as they climbed the wide stairs. The front door opened. ''Good morning, Endicott.''

Endicott? Mollie almost laughed. This was like something out of an old black-and-white movie.

''Mr. McGuire. Welcome home.''

''Thank you. This is Miss Shaw.''

''Miss.''

''Hi.'' Mollie stuck out her hand. The man took a few unsettling moments, then shook her hand—once. His uniform looked more like a tuxedo.

''Your parents are in the morning room, sir.''

''Thank you.'' Gray stepped back, letting Mollie precede him through the door, then directed her along a maze of hallways to the rear of the house. ''Are you hyperventilating yet?'' he asked quietly as they walked.

She was still contemplating her mistake with the butler, or

whatever he was called. She'd figured out too late that shaking hands with a servant probably wasn't acceptable behavior. "Not quite."

A man rose from a yellow chintz chair when they entered the room, a tall, slender man with wavy black hair and eyes almost as dark. Mollie glanced at the woman seated beside him, her gaze fixed on Mollie, her neatly styled champagne-colored hair undisturbed by the overhead fan.

"Good morning," Gray said to them. "This is Mollie Shaw. Mollie, may I present James and Gretchen McGuire."

Mollie shook hands with each of them, then waited for her cue. When Gray motioned her to a chair, she gladly took a seat. Gray sat nearby without giving his parents a hug or kiss hello. No welcome home. No we're-so-glad-you're-back greeting.

"This is a beautiful room, Mrs. McGuire." The yellow and green surroundings were warm and inviting, even if its occupants weren't.

"Thank you, Miss Shaw."

"Oh, please call me Mollie."

Mrs. McGuire nodded. "Did you have a nice flight?"

"Oh, yes! It was just wonderful. I've never flown before. I think I had my nose pressed to the window the whole time. Everything looked so small! Then we could see into everyone's yards as we came in for a landing. Does everyone have a swimming pool..." She noted the coolness in the air and stopped talking, knowing she'd been prattling out of nervousness.

"Many do, I'm sure. Where do you live?"

"Minneapolis." Gray was right, Mollie thought. There hadn't been even the tiniest change in his mother's expression.

"Mollie owns a flower shop. She designed the basket I sent you."

"Did you? It was lovely. I'll give you a tour of my gardens later, if you'd like."

"That would be wonderful. Thank you." Mollie shifted in her chair.

"I imagine you would like to freshen up a bit after your flight," Gretchen said. "James and I will be leaving for church shortly. Would you like to attend with us, darling?"

"We have plans, Mother."

He stood, so Mollie did, as well. Apparently they'd been dismissed, after a conversation shorter than Mollie might have with a browsing customer. No one had even brought up the weather, which was glorious—warm and cloudless.

"We'll see you at lunch," Gray said.

"I'll need to speak with you after," James McGuire said.

"Of course."

Mollie followed Gray silently out of the room, down a couple of halls then up some stairs. Everything gleamed, from the highly waxed, wood floors to the enormous chandelier in the entryway at the foot of the sweeping staircase. The place smelled of lemon oil, a soothing balm to Mollie's frayed nerves, even if the house itself didn't breathe warmth like Mac and Kelly's big, beautiful home. Love went a long way toward filling up empty spaces, Mollie decided.

"They put you in the room adjoining mine," Gray said, opening a door.

"Really? Why?"

"Because I requested it."

She looked around at the four-poster bed with canopy, the spindly legged lady's desk and the fine damask prints that curtained the windows and covered the bed. A bouquet of Queen Elizabeth, Peace and Sterling Silver roses welcomed her, the lovely crystal vase centered on a starched, crocheted doily.

"I'm in here." Gray opened the door connecting their rooms.

She peeked in, discovering a room similar to hers, with fabrics a little more masculine and a sturdier desk. "This wasn't your room when you were a boy?"

"I'm a guest now. I haven't lived here for more than ten years."

"Oh."

Gray watched her take in everything, watched the light fade from her eyes. He'd tried to warn her, but she probably couldn't have pictured how different his life had been from hers. Her disappointment was evident. He needed to change that. "I hope you brought shorts with you."

"Yes. Why?"

"Because you'll need them where we're going. Unless you'd rather stay here and rest up from your exhausting journey?"

She smiled at his words, then looked around her room again. "I don't see my suitcase anywhere."

"It's been unpacked for you."

"Someone put my underwear away? Eeuw. That's creepy. Not to mention the fact I'll have to hunt down where everything is."

He frowned. "I'm so used to people taking care of the details that I don't think about it anymore."

"And have those people become invisible to you?"

Which was a very good question—and one he didn't care to answer. He believed he was more distracted than pretentious, but her chiding tone hit home. "Knock on my door when you're ready."

Her eyes gleamed with challenge. "You think it'll take me longer than you to change?"

"Those are betting words, Mollie Shaw."

She tugged her blouse free and started unbuttoning from the bottom. "Winner buys hot fudge sundaes."

His attention was diverted by her fingers as they worked another button free, then another until only the top button remained, her blouse falling open slightly to reveal a hint of pale skin. "Ah, shouldn't it be the loser who buys?"

"Think about it," she said, giving him a little shove toward his room.

He didn't want to think about anything but that sliver of flesh that made his mouth water. She unfastened the top button then, but held the blouse closed. He recalled the bra he'd seen hanging over an open dresser drawer in her apartment. White. Plain. Incredibly sexy. Was that what she wore now?

"You'd better get a move on," she said as she kicked off her shoes and shimmied her panty hose down and off from under her skirt with her free hand, while holding her blouse shut with other. And there he stood, like a gawking teenager who was seeing a girl undress in front of him for the first time.

What did she think? That he was like a brother or something? A nonsexual human being? A man without needs?

He leaned against the doorjamb and crossed his arms. "I think I'll see just how far you'll go while I'm standing here."

That stopped her. "How far do you want me to go?"

Not the right answer, he thought, realizing she might accept the dare—although he doubted it. He shut the door in her face.

She made clucking sounds through the wood.

He smiled, because she couldn't see.

"Ha!" she shouted less than thirty seconds later, following it with a staccato knock. "Hot fudge sundaes are on me!"

"That doesn't make sense. Loser should pay."

"I figured it was the only way I could pay for something on this trip."

He pulled a T-shirt over his head, then intentionally slowed himself down. He'd been hurrying. Racing. "I invited you, Mollie. You're my guest."

"Which doesn't mean that you get to pay for everything. Can I come in? Are you decent?"

"Sure."

She seemed to burst in, bringing sunshine and laughter and energy. He caught her sweeping his body with an interested gaze, then she stretched out on her stomach on his bed. He debated between sneakers and a pair of soft, casual loafers he could wear without socks, which were probably more practical for where they were headed.

"I do earn a good living, you know," she said, resting her chin on her folded arms.

Living hand to mouth was a good living? He could argue the point—except that for all his money, he wasn't nearly as happy as she.

"I don't think your mother likes me," she said out of the blue.

A knock on the door saved him from answering. Mollie scampered out of his bedroom and into hers like a vapor trail. Only the quiet click of the latch indicated she'd gone. Shaking his head at her theatrical exit, he opened the hall door. "Mother. I thought you'd already left."

Gretchen strode past him and into the room. "Is everything to your liking, darling?"

"Yes, of course." He noticed she put her back to Mollie's room and kept her voice low.

"And your...friend? Is she comfortable?"

"I'm sure she is. Although she wouldn't complain, regardless."

"Yes, I could see that. She's a lovely girl. Very fresh."

Subtle emphasis on the word *girl*, Gray noted. "Yes, she is."

"And you met in Minneapolis? How did that happen?"

"She was one of the sponsors of a charity ball I attended." Which was just a little misleading. Mollie hadn't been there in person, after all. But his mother could make her own assumptions from that bit of information.

"You seem to be spending a lot of time there these days."

"Is there a point to this, Mother?"

Her last face-lift had left her with a permanently inquisitive expression, and looking younger, too, of course.

"Shouldn't I be curious about the girl my son brings home for me to meet? You've never brought an overnight guest before. Why should you? You live barely twenty minutes away."

"I wanted the two of you to spend some time together. This seemed the easiest way."

Tension sparked between them. "Don't tell me you're thinking of marrying that child?"

"Child?" An image popped into his head. Sleek, yet curvy. Long-legged. A fresh, flowery scent sometimes mixed with a hint of magic. Woman. She was all woman.

"You know what I mean." Gretchen lowered her voice further. "She wouldn't do."

"Wouldn't do what?"

"Don't play word games with me. She wouldn't do as wife to a man with your responsibilities. Your status."

Gray angled closer to his mother so that Mollie couldn't possibly overhear, even if she had her ear pressed to the door. "I expect you to treat her with respect, Mother. She's a nice young woman who's going through a hard time. Her mother died not too long ago, and she's still grieving. I thought she would enjoy a trip to California. I thought the change of scenery would be good for her."

"Are you saying you're not considering marriage with her?"

"I'm saying I want her to feel welcome here. Like you, she loves flowers. It shouldn't be hard for you to use that common bond to make her feel at ease."

James McGuire stepped into the room. "We'll be late, Gretchen, dear."

"I'm coming." She moved smoothly toward her husband. "Luncheon at two o'clock, darling."

"We'll be there," Gray said. He glanced at his watch after they left. It didn't give them much time. Grabbing his wallet and keys, he stepped into his shoes, then knocked on Mollie's door.

"Ready?" he asked when she opened the door. She'd brushed her hair and put on some lipstick, so he guessed she hadn't been trying to listen in on the conversation.

"Absolutely. Where are we going?"

"You're going to get your first up-close look at the Pacific Ocean."

She launched herself at him. "Wishes do come true," she whispered into his neck, her breath warm.

Once again he felt like her knight, only this time he let the image linger in his mind.

Seven

"**I** feel like I missed curfew," Mollie said morosely as Gray drove the last mile to home. "I did that once. Only once. My mother was waiting at the door for us, arms crossed, foot tapping. I was grounded for two weeks."

"How late were you?"

"Well…an hour, but we had a good reason."

Gray smiled. She had probably used the same tone of righteous indignation with her mother on that fateful night. He couldn't remember being grounded for anything. Probably because he spent his free time working instead of going out with friends. He hadn't played sports or held an office or joined an on-campus club. "What was your 'good reason'?"

"We fell asleep."

"Where?"

"In his car."

"Where?"

"Well…parked by the lake, but we hadn't done anything." She flipped her hair behind her shoulder with her hand. "Not much, anyway. Didn't you ever get caught?"

"I never parked with a girl."

"Never?"

He shook his head at her incredulous tone.

"You missed out, Gray. Necking in a car is fun. It's exciting. It's dangerous," she added with a dramatic whisper. "The cops know the places the kids use, so every once in a while they sneak up alongside the car and flash their light in your eyes, then send you home."

"You, meaning *you?* Or *you* in the general sense?"

"The reason we were only an hour late that night was because a cop rousted us."

Rousted. Gray laughed at the scene he imagined. "I wish I'd been the one in the car with you."

"*You* would've set your watch alarm so we wouldn't be late."

He laughed again, feeling as free and easy as one of the seagulls they'd watched at the beach. He turned into the driveway and eased the car down the path, then he heard Mollie sigh, loud and deep.

"Will your parents have waited on lunch because of us being fifteen minutes late?"

"Probably."

"Great. Another reason for your mother not to like me. Not to mention the sand we're tracking in with us, which means we need to clean up first. Which will make lunch even later."

"We would have to change, regardless. Shorts are not allowed at the dining room table. Anyway, I'm the one to blame. I didn't want to leave."

He'd obeyed all the rules that Mollie had set down as they'd driven to Half Moon Bay. Serious topics were prohibited, especially anything to do with business. Computer was a forbidden word. Fun was the only order of the day. And watching her face when she stepped onto the beach for the first time, then waded into the ocean was worth any comment his mother might make.

"Is there an outside shower?" she asked. "Or a back entrance where we can sneak in?"

There were both, but he wanted his parents to see them like this—sandy, windblown, a little sunburned. Relaxed. He wanted them to hear him laugh, to enjoy the sound as much as he had the past few days. He wanted to hear his parents laugh.

If anyone could manage that feat it would be Miss Mollie Sunshine, whose hands were clenched and whose gaze was focused unwaveringly on the house.

"Don't get so worked up about this," he said as he parked the car.

"I want your mother to like me."

"I know." He came around to her side of the car and helped her brush off the sand that had dried on her legs, wishing suddenly that he'd taken her to his hotel instead. They shouldn't have had to cut short their day at the beach. He could've watched her for hours as she sifted sand between her fingers, her eyes full of wonder, her hair a fiery red under the sun, her skin flushed. She'd laughed with pure pleasure as crabs scampered across the sand and up the rocks. She'd exclaimed over seeing tiny fish swim around her ankles. If they hadn't been so rushed she might have seen a seal or two.

He would bring her back sometime.

"Good day, Endicott," Mollie said as they strolled through the open door.

"Miss."

"Don't you get Sunday off?"

"Generally so."

"So, how come you're here?"

"I didn't want to miss Mr. McGuire's visit."

Disappointed that his parents weren't on hand to see them arrive, Gray had been urging Mollie along, then stopped at the surprising declaration. "Thank you, Endicott," he said. "Thank you very much."

"I'll tell your mother you'll be along presently."

"Better give us fifteen minutes."

"Yes, sir."

Mollie had been watching Gray's face throughout the exchange. He was pleased at Endicott's words. How very little it took to make him happy, she thought. He was starved for personal attention, a personal touch. She could understand why, of course. If you didn't grow up with open affection, you didn't know how to show it. She'd touched him every chance she'd gotten at the beach, but he'd never instigated touching, always keeping his hands clenched or stuffed in his pockets, as if afraid she might reject him.

She blamed his mother for that.

"Race you to the rooms," she said under her breath as they reached the bottom step of the staircase.

He took off.

"Hey!" She followed as fast as she could, but he took the stairs three at a time, then disappeared down the hall before she made it to the top. He was holding her bedroom door open for her when she got there, panting.

"You—" she gasped "—cheated."

"You're a poor loser," he said amiably. "Break your earlier record for changing clothes, will you? But try to look composed."

Shaking her head, she laughed, appreciating the friendlier, more open Gray. She was good for him. She wondered if he recognized that.

"You must spend a lot of time out here," Mollie said to Gretchen as they strolled through the garden later.

"Almost every morning. I do love my flowers." She carried her clippers and a flat basket, snipping blossoms as they walked, setting the blooms atop the wicker. "You must, as well, being a florist."

"Oh, yes. I have to use a wholesaler, but flowers from a backyard garden smell so good. I'd like to have one of my own someday."

"How did you come to own a flower shop at so young an age?"

"My mother bought the shop when I was a baby, and I grew up there. It's all I know how to do."

"My son told me your mother passed away recently. Please accept my condolences."

"Thank you." Mollie was positive she was going to say something wrong—something to embarrass Gray—so she said as little as possible.

"My mother passed away when I was young, too. I lacked guidance after that." She looked into the horizon. "I made mistakes."

"Like what?" Horrified, Mollie immediately apologized. "I don't have the right to ask you."

"It's quite all right, my dear. Let's sit, shall we?"

They sat on a stone bench, surrounded by fragrant roses and warmed by the sun. Mollie glanced toward Gretchen, waiting, noting the differences between Gray's mother and hers. Karen would have linked arms with Mollie, buried her face in the blossoms along the way, stopping to enjoy each rose bush, whereas Gretchen merely admired and snipped. Both were slender, but Gretchen seemed…brittle. Karen's hair had once been the burnished copper of Mollie's, then had grayed attractively. Gretchen's champagne-colored hair didn't reveal one softening strand of gray. Mollie didn't have anything against hair coloring, just that the well-lacquered style only added to the woman's brittleness.

"I was lonely," Gretchen said at last. "I married a man I shouldn't have because of that loneliness."

"Gray's father?"

Her expression didn't change. "Yes."

"Gray doesn't speak of him. I know that he died, but that's all."

"I doubt Gray remembers much of him, and what he remembers is probably distorted, as children's memories often are. James has been much more of a father to him."

"He speaks respectfully of your husband."

"James is largely responsible for Gray's drive, as well as his success. He set a good example. I wish I hadn't been in such a hurry to marry. James and I are much more suited."

"But then you wouldn't have Gray."

Gretchen's face softened. "Naturally, you're right. And Gray is everything to me. Everything. There is much yet for him to accomplish."

And you aren't part of his plans. Mollie heard the words as if they'd been spoken aloud. "Mrs. McGuire, are you worried that he's about to marry me?"

She seemed genuinely startled by the question. "Oh, no. He assures me that marriage isn't on his agenda. I gather he feels sorry for you, because you lost your mother."

Pity? Perhaps that was part of his feelings for her. But not all, Mollie thought. Not all. His mother hadn't seen him playing at the beach that afternoon. Mollie had. If anyone was to be pitied, it was Gray.

"You're young. You have so much ahead of you. The anguish of your mother's death will fade in time. And I'm sure you'll meet a nice man who can buy you a house where you can grow your garden."

"And my children. At least four," Mollie added cheerfully. If Mrs. McGuire had intended to break Mollie's self-confidence, she'd failed miserably. Gray was the one who mattered. No one and nothing else did.

"Four? My. That would be a major undertaking."

"I didn't like being an only child. I want my children to have each other when something wonderful or terrible happens." Mollie gave the woman credit. She didn't defend her decision to have only one child. Instead she stood, tucked her arm through the basket and looked toward the house.

"The men will be ensconced in the office for hours yet. Is there something you'd like to do?"

"You will be attending the board of directors meeting next week?"

Gray heard his stepfather's questioning tone, but understood the command that it really was. "I'll be there." He wandered to the window, which overlooked the backyard, and saw Mollie strolling from the house to the pool. Over her shoulder lay a towel from her bathroom—which would give his mother fits in itself. She wore a deep purple swimsuit with high-cut legs and a modest neckline. Her breasts were molded by the shimmery, almost-form-fitting fabric.

She didn't test the water, but dropped her towel, sat on the side of the pool and slipped in. She'd told him earlier that she wasn't a strong swimmer, so he guessed she would stay in the shallow end and splash around. Entertaining herself seemed easy for her, while he'd always needed a computer in front of him for that.

"People have begun to express concern about how much you're away from the office these days," James said.

"Since I haven't taken a vacation in fifteen years, I think 'people' should cut me some slack." He watched Mollie jump up and down, joy in her face.

"I'm not concerned with what other people think, son. My concern is where you're spending your time."

"Minneapolis is my place of birth. I was curious."

"It was my birthplace, as well. If you have questions…"

"Thanks, but I'm finding the answers myself." He felt James come up beside him, so he moved away from the window, not wanting to share the view of Mollie playing in the pool. He recalled her race to be able to buy hot-fudge sundaes, then her remark that she made a good living.

He wished he could live as she did—day to day, simply, doing what he loved to do. Instead, he fit too much into each day, trying to stay abreast of every facet of McGuire Enterprises and the business world at large. There were social obligations, charity obligations, family obligations. He was tired of what his life had become.

What do you want? The question echoed and bounced. *Something of my own,* came the answer in a loud, clear, distinct voice.

He could hear James talking, but the words were garbled in the maelstrom in his head. He was too young to be having a midlife crisis, but he seemed to be having one of major proportions. And he didn't believe the crisis would end until he'd avenged his father—his real father—and Mollie, too.

Gray spoke over his shoulder to his stepfather as he left the room, impolitely abrupt. "If you'll excuse me, I see that Mollie is without company. She's my guest, after all." He hurried upstairs, pulled on some swim trunks, then took the servants' staircase down to the backyard.

He found her sitting on the edge of the pool, leaning back on her hands and moving her feet leisurely through the water. She knew how to relax. Her head was tipped toward the sky, the position arching her back and thrusting her breasts upward.

She saw him coming and smiled. "All done working?"

"For now." He sat beside her, feeling someone's eyes on him as he did so. James's or his mother's? Both? He could almost hear them discussing him. "I brought you a pool towel. It's over there with mine on the lounge chair."

"There are towels especially for use by the pool, huh?"

"In the cabana." He angled his head toward the glass-walled structure.

Mollie sighed.

"How was your visit with my mother?"

"Fine."

He waited, but she said nothing more, just closed her eyes and lifted her face again to the sun. He let his gaze follow every curve and plane of her lithe body, saw her nipples tighten, as if aware of his scrutiny. She arched a little more. Her skin glowed from the sunshine pouring down on her. In his mind's eye her suit disappeared.

Gray got hard just watching, so he slipped into the pool. Lap after lap he swam, not counting how many times he turned and pushed off, not caring, fed up with holding back his need for her, wishing he didn't know everything he knew about her—and glad that he did.

He pushed off again, stronger, swifter, remembering the look on his stepfather's face when he reminded Gray of his responsibilities. As if he were the royal heir to the throne.

He was heir to a different throne, one he wanted so badly he was willing to go public with accusations against one of the country's most sterling citizens, accusations of professional thievery and personal immorality against a man who would have the full support of the powerful Fortune family.

Gray chopped the water with a hypnotic windmill of arms. His legs burned. He focused on the pain, as relentless as his need to feel it. Another lap. One more. Oblivion could be reached eventually. He crashed into something. Not the wall. Something soft.

Hands cupped his shoulders, imprisoning him.

"Stop," Mollie said softly, her mouth close to his ear. "Just stop." She felt his body go limp, then his feet touch bottom. He was the most complicated person she knew, locking so much inside himself. What demon drove him? Had his father said something to upset him? Did he disapprove of Mollie, too, like his mother?

"Sorry," Gray said, shifting so that he rested his back against the side of the pool, next to her, his breathing short and shallow.

"Don't apologize. Not to me." She angled toward him, wanting to distract him. Be fearless, she told herself. "Your body is perfect."

He made a noise as if denying her words.

"You could be a model," she insisted. "An underwear model."

His laugh came out ragged, but at least he laughed. He ran a hand through his hair, shoving it back.

"It's true. Your face is really interesting. Your shoulders are broad. Your chest is, um, well, it's incredible. You've got amazingly narrow hips and gorgeous, long legs. And you're not hairy."

He really laughed then, sinking into the water, making bubbles as he drifted all the way under before coming slowly back up, his eyes alight with humor. "I guess I'm glad you noticed."

"I've been noticing from the moment you stepped into my shop."

"So have I. Been noticing you, that is."

If they entered into a more intimate relationship, would that ruin everything? she wondered. Would he fire her as the party planner if they stopped being—dare she say it?—lovers? The party was inconsequential in comparison.

"Excuse me, sir. Miss."

She hadn't seen or heard Endicott approach, but Gray didn't show any signs of being surprised.

"Yes, Endicott?" he asked.

"I'm to remind you that dinner is at seven, sir."

"What time is it now?"

"Five past six."

"Thank you. We'll be on time."

Mollie winked at the stiff-backed butler. "He's afraid she'll ground him."

"Yes, miss." Endicott bowed, then left.

"He winked at me," Mollie said as she climbed the steps out of the pool.

"Endicott did?"

"Uh-huh. You had to be looking closely."

"More closely than I was, I guess." He swept the towels off the lounge chair and laid one over Mollie's shoulders.

She tugged it closer, then sighed. "I don't suppose we'll be spending the evening playing charades with your parents."

"I don't suppose."

"What will we do?"

"Plead exhaustion from jet lag and retire early." He rubbed himself with his towel, then crouched in front of her and dried her legs.

Speechless for a moment, she laid a hand on his shoulder for balance. "How early?"

"Shall we synchronize our watches? How about nine o'clock?"

"Do you think they'll decide we've gone to bed early so that we can, you know, sleep together?"

Gray heard the strain in her voice. She needed to know his intentions. He'd been vague with her, because so little was clear to him. He stood. "You have a vivid imagination, Mollie Shaw."

"I'm putting two and two together, as I think they will."

His gaze dropped to her mouth. "We haven't even kissed."

"Feel free to correct that situation."

He touched a finger to her chin and angled his head, moving closer—

A quiet clearing of someone's throat intruded into the anticipation. They looked toward the house at the same time. Endicott pointed to his watch, then disappeared through the doorway.

"Our guardian angel," Mollie said.

"Our Lucifer," Gray muttered.

Eight

Doused with a fresh spritz of perfume, Mollie waited an hour after they retired to their rooms before she finally gave up on Gray and went to bed. No knock on the adjoining door made her heart kick into overdrive. No turn of the handle sent her stomach somersaulting. She waited for a first kiss that never came. Apparently she would be made to wait until his next visit to Minneapolis, since the plan was for her to take a commercial flight home the next night, alone.

She closed her eyes, tired enough to sleep, but letting the anticipation drain from her mind and body. After a while she felt herself drifting. Floating. Falling...

Click. The latch of a doorknob stopped her mid-flight. She kept her eyes closed, sensing him moving closer, but not hearing him. After a minute he pulled the sheet over her shoulders and tucked the fabric around her. She rolled onto her back, seeing him easily in the moon glow through her window. He wore sweatpants, but his chest was bare.

"I'm sorry," he said quietly. "I didn't mean to wake you."

"I was awake."

He sat beside her.

Freeing an arm from under the sheet, she wrapped her hand around his wrist. "Can't you sleep?" She sat up, knowing her nightgown covered her as completely as a T-shirt. He couldn't accuse her of tempting him.

He shook his head. "I haven't been in this house for more than a few hours at a time since I moved out more than ten years ago. I had forgotten how silent it is."

Silent. An interesting word choice, Mollie thought. Most people would have said *quiet*. "Your parents seem very settled."

"They've always been settled. No ups. No downs. No anger. No joy. Keep it cool. Stay calm. Be polite. I didn't remember that until I brought you into it. And the reason I noticed is because being here changed you."

"In what way?"

"Your brightness output dimmed."

"I can't say I've been completely at ease, Gray, but I haven't felt stifled. You seem to be testing them, though. Seeing how far you can go."

"Like some teenager," he said, pushing himself off the bed, moving toward the window.

"You're on a quest."

"Is that a nice way of saying I've gone crazy?"

"No." She watched him shove his hands into his pockets, recalling that he'd done the same thing when he'd greeted his parents. *Don't touch.* She knew now where that warning had come from, how long he'd lived with it. She wanted to put her arms around him and hold him close. To comfort. To tell him everything would be all right.

"You're searching for something." For the childhood you lost, Mollie thought, suddenly sure of it. "Something you miss. Your father?"

"When my mother married James, part of the deal was that he could adopt me, because he couldn't have children of his own." He rested his palms on the window frame and looked out at the night. "He nurtured my God-given talents. Gave me opportunities I might not have had otherwise. I owe him."

Nurtured? Nurturing meant caring, loving and showing affection. How could he think that James had nurtured him?

She and Gray couldn't think more differently, Mollie decided, a fact that should have deterred her but didn't. If anything, she cared even more deeply about him.

"You forfeited your father's name and history, which hurt you."

He angled a shoulder against the wall and crossed his arms. "The way you feel about your mom is how I felt about my dad. He was the best. Good and kind. Fun-loving. He always had time for me. We did a lot together—fishing, playing ball, tinkering with the car. People came and went constantly at our house, stayed for meals. And he always tucked me in bed, kissed me good night."

"That changed after your mother remarried."

"More than you would believe. James has been good to me, although not the same as my dad. I do feel an obligation to him. He's always treated me as his own."

"Parents shouldn't make their children feel obligated, Gray. They should just love them."

He padded across the room and sat beside her, murmuring her name so softly and with such wonder that she could hardly breathe. "I don't know what to do about you," he said. "Everything is so clear to you."

"Not always, but I'm a simple person, Gray, with simple needs."

"I'm not."

"I know that. Something is tearing you up inside." She knelt before him, needing to touch him, waiting for him to need her in the same way. She finally touched his clenched fist.

He reached for her, groaning her name, and then he kissed her.

She'd been kissed before, but not like this. Nothing like this. He wrapped his arms around her, dragging her against him as he plundered her mouth, and only her mouth, in a kiss that went on forever, it seemed. Forever. He was her forever. She'd known it the minute he'd walked into her shop. Now her fate was sealed.

He lowered her to the bed, then flattened his body on hers, still kissing her, a beggar feasting at a banquet. He tasted hot and wild and hungry. She could feel him down low, hard, blissfully hard for her. Needing him closer she wrapped her legs around his hips and arched to meet him. He reared up, sucked in a harsh breath.

She wasn't coherent. His mouth fastened on hers again, stopping the words she attempted, pulling new sounds from her that she didn't recognize. His skin was moist under her hands as she dragged them down his back, feeling his muscles bunch. Nothing about him was soft—except his lips skimming her neck, then journeying slowly back up to her mouth. This wasn't just a first kiss, but a lifetime kiss. Promise and fulfillment. Now and always. Nothing had prepared her for the escalating sensations, for her total abandonment, for the love that crushed her heart. Was it really possible to love someone that fast?

He dragged his mouth from hers, then held himself motionless, his breath ragged. Rolling onto his side, he cupped the back of her head and pressed her face against his chest, the gesture so tender, it made her eyes and throat burn. Love and joy and confusion bubbled inside her.

"You don't do anything halfway," she said, as he pulled her leg over his hip, bringing their lower bodies back in contact. She felt him, still flatteringly hard. "I didn't know a kiss could feel like that. Could do all that to me."

"You've been one surprise after another, as well," Gray said in the understatement of the century. He'd been blindsided by her response—by the way she'd pushed her hips off the bed, not only meeting his but forcing a rhythm he'd had to break. Who would've guessed Miss Mollie Sunshine was combustible enough to shoot fire directly into his body?

Moving back a little, he grabbed the sheet and pulled it over her, needing to put a barrier between them, needing to defuse the urgency, to think about something else, something to ice down his need. "I have to go into the office tomorrow," he said. "If you don't mind coming with me, I can take care of the most essential business, then we can scout potential locations for the anniversary party."

She took her time answering, as if his words were in a foreign language requiring translation. "You sure can turn it off as fast as you turn it on," she grumbled, turning her back to him, flouncing a little.

He heard the blunt tone of voice, the accusation that lingered. She was wrong. He wanted her. Ached with wanting her. But he wouldn't make love to her in his parents' house.

He climbed out of the bed, once again wishing he'd taken her to his hotel, instead—and grateful he hadn't. Had he really known her only five days?

When he reached the doorway, he turned. "Do you want me to leave the door open?"

"I'm not afraid of the dark."

His mouth twitched at her indignant tone.

"I don't have nightmares, either," she continued, "so you don't have to worry about coming in here in the middle of the night to comfort me."

He grinned. Sparring with her had become the highlight of his life. "I'll shut the door, then." He grabbed the knob.

"It isn't fair," she complained.

"What isn't?"

"You come in here and get me all riled up, then off you go, not a care in the world! You came, you kissed, you left."

"I was as *riled up* as you. Men can't hide that. What do you want from me, Mollie?"

She sighed. "I don't know."

The intricacies of her mind intrigued him. "Stopping was the right thing to do," he said.

"I suppose. Good night."

He didn't lie down but stared out his bedroom window for a long time, contemplating the hole he'd dug for himself. He'd pursued the downfall of Stuart Fortune without letting consequences block his path. Now Mollie sat squarely in the middle of the narrowing road. He couldn't step over or around her on the final leg. She would need to be beside him.

Hell, he needed her, too. When the end came, they might have *only* each other, all bridges burned behind them.

Only each other. Something of my own. The phrases danced a bit, then mingled. Merged. Burned.

Finally he slept.

"Marry me."

The air between Gray and Mollie snapped and crackled. They were seated in his car at the private airstrip where they'd landed the day before. It was 6:00 p.m. He'd canceled her commercial flight home in the middle of the night when he'd come to his decision to propose.

"What?" Mollie asked, her voice filled with the same shock reflected on her face.

He was amazed at his calmness. Everything was clear now. Stuart Fortune had to fall, but his tumble would throw Mollie's life into a tailspin. She would need protection from the inevitable pain and disillusionment ahead of her when she learned that Stuart was her father—and protection was something Gray could provide. When the press moved in, he would build a fort around her, keeping her safe, something her father should have done.

But marriage is for life.

Yeah. So?

"Marry me," he said, more insistently, ignoring the voice in his head. "We can stop in Las Vegas on the way back to Minneapolis."

"You can't be serious."

"Serious, sober and not asking out of sexual frustration, in case you're wondering. Although that's part of it." If she needed coaxing, he would coax. But she was alone in the world and earned barely enough to support herself. She could accept his proposal for security and companionship, if nothing else, as his mother had with his stepfather. Experience had taught Gray that marriage wasn't only for the love-struck. Other reasons mattered. She wanted a family so much she could taste it. She'd said so.

"I can't leave you alone, I admit that. We rile each other up, and the tension will become unbearable. But there's more, Mollie. It feels right. Everything about it feels right."

She stared at him for a long time. "I need to think about this," she said, finally, her voice strained.

"Take your time. I'll take the luggage to the plane."

Mollie watched him walk away from the car a minute later, a suitcase in each hand. He disappeared into the jet, not looking back, not hesitating. Exactly how much time did she have to make this life-altering decision?

She should have insisted on knowing his reasons other than that it "feels right." Why hadn't she asked why he proposed?

Do you really want the answer to that?

She entwined her fingers. Maybe not. She was more than a little in love with him, but he hadn't mentioned the word— although he probably couldn't verbalize it anyway, given his upbringing. He hardly touched her beyond what courtesy required, unless they were kissing. She rubbed her temples, concentrating on the bigger picture.

Surely he wouldn't propose marriage, a lifetime commitment, without loving her a little?

Hopeless romantic. The words taunted her. She pushed her hair out of her face, then rested her hands against the back of her neck. There was no one in her life to object or consent to the marriage. Except for the fact they'd known each other less than a week, she couldn't think of any reason to say no. Some explanation existed for why she'd obsessed about his photograph in the newspaper. And there was some rationalization for why he'd come so coincidentally into her life. Maybe there was such a thing as destiny. Or maybe angels could assist mortals, after all.

It could be that he'd been sent to her specifically so that his life would change from something sterile and all-business to one of warmth and affection and love, which he seemed to be starving for. A lot of people recognized his analytical and brilliant mind, his power and status. But had anyone recognized how lonely he was? Or were his eyes mirrors reflecting her own loneliness, her own hunger for someone to love and for someone to love her. Her need to raise her own family—with both a mother and father.

She wanted to belong to him, body and soul. She wanted the right to touch him, to hold him, to be held.

She saw him then, standing in the open hatch of the plane,

waiting. He wasn't making this easy on her. She wished he would come open the car door, take her hand and help her out, then guide her straight into his arms. She wished he would tell her he loved her, needed her. Was his wanting her enough for now? A line from her mother's journal popped into her mind: "I shouldn't have married him thinking I would change him."

Karen had found out the hard way that people don't change, except to reveal more weaknesses. Yet, Gray wasn't cruel like her mother's husband had been. He wouldn't hurt her. The worst that could happen would be that he never opened up emotionally. Could she live with that?

Oh, she wanted to try. She had so much love inside her, all bundled up and waiting to burst out and straight into him. She wanted to fill him with love and tenderness and laughter. She wanted his life to be bright and happy, everything that it hadn't been. She wanted the chance to show him that nurturing meant caring, loving unconditionally, being there through good times and bad, not expecting more than he could give.

Pollyanna. A rebellious inner voice muttered the word in an exasperated tone.

Mollie opened the car door, shut it firmly behind her, then walked to the plane. Up the stairs. He waited, his gaze on hers, patient, gentle, with barely a flicker of anticipation—or was it wariness?—in his eyes.

She stopped on the top step. He didn't move to let her pass by.

"I love you," she said. Undaunted by how he stiffened, she took his hands in hers. "Yes, I'll marry you."

Nine

Her declaration of love sliced through Gray's equilibrium like a guillotine. Words eluded him. How could she love him when she didn't know him? She must have given him a starring role in some romantic fantasy—and the death of any fantasy was brutal, particularly to someone young and trusting and lonely. He knew that better than most, he supposed.

Being a practical man, he knew he couldn't return those fantasy feelings. Being a man of conscience—toward Mollie, at least—he knew he should rescind the proposal rather than put her through everything he had planned, particularly now that she fantasized herself being in love. Conscience or practicality? Which carried the most weight?

The decision was taken out of his hands when she smiled at him, her eyes warm and welcoming, her tender hands touching him, offering comfort and peace. So he kissed her, knowing she needed to hear words of love in return, knowing they weren't in him to say. Love was too fleeting, too fragile, too risky. Risk didn't belong in personal relationships.

But hope drifted around him like a feather floating and tickling and brushing against his heart as Mollie snuggled against him after the kiss ended.

"We need to get up in the air," he said, distracted by the scent of her hair, which oddly aroused and relaxed him at the same time. Not only would he get to make love with her, he would get to sleep beside her. All night. Every night.

She preceded him into the plane and immediately took her seat. He left her to buckle herself in as he opened the cockpit door to speak to the pilot, then he took a folder from his briefcase, sat beside her and met her gaze. Starry-eyed. He finally knew what that meant.

"I have a few questions," she said.

"Go ahead."

"Am I part of your rebellion?"

The plane rumbled as it moved toward the runway. "Meaning?"

"You know your mother won't approve of me as your wife. Is that why you asked?"

"No." He leaned toward her. "Absolutely not." Or was it...?

She sat silent for a minute, then said, "I don't want to give up my shop."

He took note of her defensive tone. "I won't ask you to. But I hope you'll let me help you make it easier to run. And I hope you'll hire some help."

"I'd already decided to do that, with or without your input. I've got interviews set up for tomorrow with three women who've come by looking for work since Mom died."

The plane gathered speed, then lifted. They were airborne.

"I'm afraid I could get used to this life of luxury," she said, looking out the window. "I suppose I should have asked this question before I said yes to your proposal, but where will we live?"

"Not in California. I resigned as CEO today." So far, only his stepfather knew, but he would announce it to the board of directors next week.

One week closer to freedom.

"Good," Mollie said, squeezing his hand, her face serious. "That job was killing your soul."

He had a soul? "It'll take a few months before I can abdicate all responsibility, not counting the time my parents will spend trying to change my mind. I'll be linked to the company forever, anyway, because of my software designs, but I intend to settle in Minneapolis. I'm moving forward on my plans for that company I told you about."

"What kind of business is it?"

He hesitated. Would she recognize it as a Fortune company? He needed to know the answer to that question. "It's called Knight Star Systems. They design and manufacture security systems."

When she didn't show signs of recognition, he opened the folder, withdrew a sheet of paper and passed it to her. "I started on the wedding arrangements."

She sat back in the seat, surprise in her pretty green eyes. "When?"

"While you were touring McGuire Enterprises earlier today."

"You were that confident?"

"If it was going to happen today in Las Vegas, I had to be prepared. Nothing was done that couldn't be undone."

Mollie read the neatly typed notes, wishing she could cuddle up next to him. This was beginning to feel like a business deal. Which, she reminded herself, was one of the reasons why she was marrying him. He needed her to balance his dreary, business side.

"You can call the florist from here and tell her what you want," he said, making notes in the margins of his own paperwork. "The next number connects you with a woman who will try to track down a dress to your liking."

Mollie shook her head and laughed softly.

He looked up. "What's the joke?"

"Don't you find it just a little ironic that the wedding planner doesn't get to plan her own wedding?"

"I didn't commit to anything. I just researched and lined up people, just in case. You'll get to make all the choices."

"Las Vegas." She sighed. "I hope the wedding won't be at a place with Elvis in neon lights."

He smiled. "It's a chapel on the strip, but it's one used by people who require confidentiality. We should be able to announce the marriage ourselves, instead of the press treating it like a circus. Only the best for you, Mollie Sunshine.''

Mollie Sunshine? Oh, she liked that. "The chapel is famous for confidentiality?'' she asked. "But the paparazzi haven't caught on?''

He grinned.

She rubbed her face with her hands. "Your father probably hates me. The way I figure it, he blames me for you quitting. And your mother is going to die. She'll be furious at being excluded from the plans. I'm sure she wanted a big, splashy, society wedding, like the one I'm planning for Chloe Fortune and Mason Chandler.''

"She liked you.''

"How could you tell?'' Mollie dialed the first number. "Her expression never changed.''

"I know her better than you. I could tell.''

"Liar,'' she said cheerfully, then she got busy doing what she loved best—planning a wedding.

Gray hung up the phone and glanced at Mollie as she tapped her pen against her lips. She was focused on the paperwork in front of her, a page littered with check marks and handwritten notations, like his.

He wanted this wedding to be memorable for her, something she wouldn't be embarrassed to recall. Something she wouldn't regret. She might regret the marriage eventually, but not the wedding itself. So the music needed to be right, the setting elegant, the clothing suited to the occasion. And flowers. She needed flowers.

"May I have a clean piece of paper?'' she asked, looking up.

As soon as he handed her one, she bent over it, intent on what she was writing. After a few minutes he glanced at his watch. They should be touching down soon. Within a couple of hours they would be husband and wife. Why wasn't he panicking?

"You need to sign this.'' She thrust a piece of paper toward him.

Written on top were the words "Prenuptial Agreement.'' He

skimmed the concise list: (1) Gray McGuire will hold no financial interest in Every Bloomin' Thing; (2) Mollie Shaw will hold no financial interest in McGuire Enterprises, Knight Star Systems or any other business held now or in the future by Gray McGuire; (3) Gray McGuire will not expect Mollie Shaw to live in a mansion or employ servants. Endicott may come live with us and become part of our family, if he chooses, however.

Gray smiled at that before he continued reading: (4) Gray McGuire will make no major decisions that would affect Mollie Shaw without consulting her first; (5) children of this union will be provided for but will not be given large sums of money at any time in their lives.

She'd drawn three lines, one with the date, one she had signed and one left blank for his signature.

"I'm a simple person, with simple needs," she'd said last night, and her idea of a prenuptial agreement reflected that simplicity, that uncluttered view of the world. Faith in the world.

He wished he felt the same.

"This won't hold up in court," he said gently.

"Why does that matter? It's between you and me. I don't expect to see you in court."

He pulled out another folder from his briefcase and passed it to her, a generic document his lawyer had drawn up years ago—just in case. "This is the one we need to sign."

"I guess you *are* prepared." She flipped through the pages. "Okay. I'll sign this if you'll sign mine."

"You should read it first, Mollie."

"Why? I trust you or else I wouldn't be marrying you."

His stomach clenched. "You should know what you're signing."

"Is there anything in here that my own lawyer would object to?"

"He would want more financial guarantees for you."

"Which, as my paper clearly indicates, I don't want." She waited, her pen poised over the signature line on the last sheet of the twelve-page document.

"You can't sign it yet. We'll need witnesses."

"Well, no witnesses are required for mine." Her gaze was direct and unwavering.

"I didn't realize you were this stubborn," he muttered with some humor as he scrawled his name on her document.

"You wouldn't want to marry someone you could manipulate too easily, would you?" she asked, tucking the paper into her purse dramatically.

"I don't suppose I would."

"Good." She maneuvered herself into his lap. "Enough business. We're about to be married. I need a kiss."

She didn't wait for him to take the initiative but kissed him first. With a growl he tipped her back, turning the kiss into an attack as she laughed against his mouth, the laughter fading as the kiss deepened.

"Thank you for marrying me," he said after a minute, stroking her hair back from her face.

She brushed her fingertips across his lips. "I love you. Don't thank me for that."

A tone chimed. Saved by the bell. "That means we're about to land."

"I remember," she said, accepting his help to climb off his lap. She buckled herself into the next seat. "Mollie McGuire," she mused. "It has a nice ring, doesn't it?"

"Your Irish leprechaun would agree."

"Oh! Yarg. I forgot." She laughed. "You don't like him much, do you?"

"I dream about melting his voice chip." The plane touched down with a soft bounce, then glided smoothly as it slowed. "We're here." Again he waited for panic to set in. But there was only peace.

She'd left her hair down. Her dress was simple and elegant and...*her,* a cream-colored silk sheath topped by a short-sleeved chiffon jacket.

Gray watched Mollie start down the short aisle, her bouquet shaking, her eyes large and luminous. Pale pink lipstick drew his gaze to her mouth. She smiled. Sort of.

He left his spot to walk to her, offering his arm. She rested her cheek against him for a moment and whispered her thanks. Her perfume reached him, the same, yet different. Always different.

He was so aware of her. Of her quiet voice as she repeated the vows, of the squeeze of her hand as he repeated his. *Human sparkler,* he thought once again as she elbowed him, her eyes laughing when, distracted by the anticipation of making love with her later, he didn't respond immediately to the man asking for the ring.

He slid the emerald-and-diamond symbol of their marriage onto her finger, then he kissed the soft, sweet spot above it. When he straightened, he saw her eyes glisten and her chin notch a little higher. She aimed a gold band for his finger; he helped to guide it on. Tenderness overwhelmed him. He was asking so much of her—a wedding without her friends, no avowal of love from him, an instant and complete change to her life. She'd been granted no period of adjustment. No time to reconsider. She would need his protection. He needed to give it. How could he explain it to her when the time came? What words would help?

"You may kiss the bride."

Sweet words, indeed. And enough for now.

It was almost midnight when they arrived at Mollie's shop.

"I thought we were coming here so you could put your bouquet in the refrigerator case," he said as they climbed the stairs to her apartment.

"On our way out." Anticipation of what would happen soon made her legs a little wobbly. "I just need to pick up a few things to take with me." A change of underwear, her dusting powder, her bathrobe for the morning. The hotel probably provided one, but she needed the comfort of her own.

She didn't want to take off her beautiful, beautiful dress. And Gray had given her emerald-and-diamond earrings and a pendant before the ceremony, then added a matching wedding band at the proper moment, which felt heavy and hot on her finger— his personal brand, his public declaration that she was his, forever. She lifted her bouquet to her face and sniffed the white and peach roses. She hated leaving it behind, even just for the night. But if she wanted to preserve it, she needed to handle it right.

Flipping on lights, Mollie walked to her bedroom and set her bouquet on her nightstand. She opened a dresser drawer and stared blindly at the contents. Gray's hands settled on her shoulders. She jumped.

He rubbed her arms until she rested against him, her head cupped by the hollow of his shoulder, her back pressed to his hard chest.

"Are you nervous?" he asked.

"Kind of. More excited than nervous, I think."

"Be fearless, Mollie McGuire."

"I'm trying." She relaxed a little more, enjoying hearing her new name said aloud by someone else for the first time.

His arms encircled her. His cheek pressed against hers. "I know it's been a lot to absorb in one day. If you'd rather spend the night here, I would understand."

"No!" She turned in his arms. "I want to be with you."

He gave her the most tender look she'd seen from him. "I meant that we could stay here tonight. If it would be easier for you. It's familiar. Maybe it would help."

"There are only twin beds." She looked at her bed with its utterly feminine, flowered bedspread and pillows. She couldn't picture him there.

"I don't think the size of the bed matters tonight, Sunshine." He pressed his lips to her temple. Her legs went weak.

"I...I want to take a shower."

"Fine."

"I don't have anything beautiful to wear. I should've bought something in Las Vegas. I wasn't thinking ahead."

"I was." His lips toyed with hers, separated them. His tongue dipped into her mouth, lingering until she returned the caress. "I was picturing you naked, not wearing something I'd have to rip right off anyway."

"Oh." She was amazed that he wanted her that much. Compared to anyone he'd been with before, she was bound to seem awkward.

He unfastened the three fabric-covered buttons on her chiffon jacket, sliding it down her arms to drape over the back of a chair.

Turning her back to him, she took off her earrings. "Would you unfasten the pendant, please?"

His fingertips feathered her skin, then the glide of the chain teased her, as well, as he pulled it away. He dragged the zipper of her dress down, down, down, ever so slowly, peeled back the fabric and kissed her shoulder blade, her spine. He trailed his tongue down that dividing line—

"Gray?"

"Hmm?"

His breath dusted her skin, sending shivers down her.

"Um, remember the first e-mail you sent me? About how you wanted to be my first?"

He made a sound she took to mean he remembered.

"This is kind of the same situation."

She felt him straighten behind her. His arms came around her waist. She wished she could stay in his embrace forever.

"It's my wedding gift to you," she said into the quiet moment, feeling his reaction in the way he held her, in the way his breathing changed, in the way his skin warmed.

"Thank you," he said, so softly she could barely hear the words, but the tone...

The tone told her so much more. Her virginity was physical, but his was emotional. Her loss of innocence would pale compared to his, when he realized he loved her.

If he loved her.

She took a step forward. "I won't take long," she said, breathless, intending to barricade herself in the bathroom until her nerves settled. Maybe they needed to be at his hotel, after all, someplace impersonal, someplace where her mother's voice couldn't follow her, asking impertinent questions about why she'd done this rash thing. Hadn't Mollie learned anything from Karen's experience?

"I'm not you," Mollie said into the shower spray. "I married a good, strong man who may not love me yet but who will. I didn't make a mistake."

The one-sided conversation calmed her—until she was tow-eled off, powdered and perfumed, when she couldn't stall a second longer. She'd forgotten to bring her robe in with her. On the back of the bathroom door hung a cotton nightie. She started to reach for it; instead, she wrapped a dry towel around her.

Darkness greeted her when she opened the door. All the lights were off. She took the few steps to her bedroom and pushed open the door. Flickering candlelight lured her closer to the bed, where her husband stood, waiting for her, wearing only his suit slacks, looking tall, dark and handsome beyond her imaginings.

Her husband. Hers. All hers.

He extended his hand toward her. She slipped hers into his, felt the warmth and strength and comfort.

"This is lovely," she said, indicating the candles, then she noticed rose petals strewn across her sheet.

"I borrowed from the shop a little. You'll have to bill me for the roses."

She was grateful she didn't have an order to fill first thing in the morning. The thought made her smile.

He nudged her hair aside and nibbled on her earlobe. "What are you smiling about?"

Her skin rose in bumps as his tongue touched the skin below her ear. "I'm happy."

"It wasn't your I'm-happy smile."

"I have different smiles?"

"Hmm. I'm waiting for the woman-as-sex-goddess one before I go on."

She laughed. "I have one of *those?*"

"You used it freely last night. And successfully." Gray tipped her head back and kissed her. She came up on tiptoe to meet him, wrapping her arms around his neck and pulling herself more snugly to him. He ran his hands down her back, curved them over her rear, lifted her to him, the terry cloth bunching in his palms. The towel inched down her body, but he resisted the urge to tug it off. Slowly, he cautioned himself. Don't startle—

"Oh, no," she said.

He counted to five. She'd already stalled once by taking a shower. How many more diversions could she create? "Oh, no?"

"I'm not on the Pill. Do you have something, you know, in your wallet?"

"No." The word simmered. On the night he most wanted everything to go right, little seemed to.

"I want a family, Gray. Now or later, it doesn't matter to me. But if you want to wait awhile, we can't do this now. My periods are really irregular, and I don't have a clue whether or not I'm ovulating."

The first shared intimacy of their marriage, Gray thought. And the first big dilemma. "I'm willing to risk it." *And I'm not willing to wait.*

Her woman-as-sex-goddess smile settled everything. He pulled her against him and closed his eyes, fighting the need to plunder. She was his wife, and she'd never made love before. But he was done with delays.

He breathed her name, knowing he should say more.

"I love you," she whispered back instantly. "I want you."

Her towel and his slacks jumbled and twined on the way to the floor, then they were skin to skin, body to body, murmuring words that never became sentences, uttering sighs that spoke of need, not contentment. No matter how many times he told himself to slow down, he couldn't remember to. Her slender body held all the right curves. Her restless hands returned every arousing caress. He sat on the edge of the bed, encouraging her to straddle him so that he could finally put his mouth to her breasts. She arched back as he kneaded her soft flesh, sucked a hard peak into his mouth. She curved her hands up his head as he shifted to the other side, held him there as she rose and fell against him, tiny movements yielding big results. The sounds she made flattered him, pleased him, aroused him beyond anything in his memory.

"Oh, this is wonderful," she said, rising up, then kissing him, her mouth hotly sweet, dangerously demanding. "Your skin burns me. Burns me. I love how you feel pressed against me—" she lifted her head and stared at him as she lowered herself to his thighs and moved her hips forward "—here."

"You make me forget everything." He muttered the words between fierce, delirious kisses.

"Except me…"

"There's only you, Sunshine. Nothing, no one but you." He shifted her to lie down, covered her body with his and found her hot, open mouth again, discovering a little more desperation in the way she sought him back, her demands growing more wild, more insistent, more frantic. Easing back, he cupped her breast, explored the tight, taut nipple, then dragged his hand down her until she went perfectly still, anticipation hardening her body. He grazed her with a fingertip. Her moan convinced him to slow down. She tipped up her pelvis as he explored her, discovered her, finding her ready for more. More. He wanted to give her so much more. Pleasure and ecstasy and satisfaction beyond her expectations.

"Don't make me wait any longer," she said, hoarse and demanding. "I want to know how you feel."

He moved over her, held himself levered above her. "Guide me."

She wrapped her hand around him for the first time. He gritted his teeth, not wanting the moment to end, afraid it would end too soon.

"You feel so wonderful," she breathed as she caressed him, tortured him with tentative strokes that turned bolder, more curious. Perilous.

"Inside, Mollie," he managed to say. "Before I lose what little control I have left."

Nothing had ever felt so good, so right, so perfect as the fit he found with her. Snug and smooth, she surrounded him like velvet. He pushed slowly, steadily, reminding her to relax, enjoying the feel of her opening to him, glorying in the singular privilege of being her first lover, wishing he could know what she felt. Wishing she could know how he felt, sheathed by her. They merged and mingled, fused. Incinerated. The moment he felt her climax peak, he spilled luxuriously into her as she cried out, in pleasure, he hoped, not pain. He didn't wait for her to come down completely before he kissed her, with great passion and gratitude and amazement at the rare gift she was.

"My husband," she said on a sigh, running her hands down his back, up his sides, her fingers tracing his ribs.

Husband. Partner. Lover. Protector. He wanted to be all things to her, this gentle, loving woman who deserved so much more than she'd had in life, all the things her father should have provided financially, at least. Gray had found her because he was seeking justice, but out of that need had come an equally strong desire to protect. And now he could never knowingly cause her pain.

He trembled inside. The fact that Stuart Fortune was her father would be Gray's secret forever. She didn't need Stuart now, anyway. She had a husband, one who would fill all the roles in her life, give her the security her father should have given her. Give her the life she deserved. And as soon as he took his father's company back from the man who stole it, Gray would give her babies and a home with a garden.

"I love you," she said softly as they lay with legs tangled, their breathing almost normal.

"I hope I didn't hurt you."

Disappointed, Mollie sent her hopefulness back into her heart. He would learn to love her, to say the words and believe them, even if he'd never heard the words from anyone before. "I'm so glad I waited for you."

"Waited for marriage, you mean."

She snuggled more comfortably against him, the limited size of the bed forcing them close, which was fine with her, especially since he had to keep his arms around her. His hands didn't stay idle, but caressed her lightly, constantly. He was already learning to touch. "You don't believe in fate?" she asked. "You don't think you were chosen for me—and I for you?"

"I think there are reasons for everything. I don't believe those reasons are written in the stars."

"Oh, you and your analytical mind. Gray, how else can you explain our meeting? What were the chances, really, given how different we are, how differently we live?"

"There's a logical explanation."

She angled away enough to see his serious face, then she grinned. "No way. There isn't a reason on earth why our paths should have crossed."

"Of course there is. The reason that brought me into your shop in the first place."

"Nope."

"Why not?"

"Because there are experienced and convenient party planners where your parents live. You picked *me*."

"Is that why you married me, Mollie? Because you believe we were fated to be together?"

"Yes, I believe that. What's your excuse? Why did you ask me to marry you?"

Gray could see she wasn't going to let the issue rest until she got an answer that satisfied her need for Karma or Kismet, or whatever she thought had drawn them together in the first place.

"See? You can't come up with a reason, either, except what you said on the plane. 'It feels right,' you said. 'Everything about it feels right.' Not logical at all, but emotional. Fate," she repeated with a self-assured nod, then she kissed him.

"I don't suppose a wedding night is the time to be debating," he said, threading his fingers through her hair.

"Probably not. Can you think of something else to do?"

Pert. She was definitely being pert. "I figured we would sleep."

"I'm sure we will. At some point."

"Mollie, you can't be ready for a second time."

"Actually," she said conspiratorially, "I'm starving. For something to eat, that is."

"Your refrigerator never has much in it."

"It has Popsicles, mint-chocolate-chip ice cream and frozen burritos."

"Burritos? Seriously?" He didn't want to lose the warmth of her body pressed to his, or the scent of rainbows and clover and heather that had seeped into his skin. "In the absence of champagne, I suppose ice cream will do."

"Stay here. I'll get it."

Ah. It was an excuse to take a few minutes for herself. Why hadn't he considered that she would need some privacy to let the experience settle a bit?

He watched her hurry out of the room too fast for him to

enjoy looking at her body, which made him wonder if he should put his briefs back on.

Compromising, he pulled the sheet to his waist as he sat up and rested his back against some pillows jammed against the headboard.

After about ten minutes, she returned, wearing a long T-shirt or nightgown, one that almost reached her knees. She carried a bowl in each hand, passing him one as she sat facing him. Tucked under her arm was a piece of newsprint that she slid across the sheet toward him. "Here's why I married you so fast."

Ten

"It wasn't fast for me," she went on, her voice quavering the tiniest bit. "I started falling in love with you over a month ago when I saw this picture in the paper."

He remembered seeing the shot in the *StarTribune* the day after the charity ball. He had to look at the caption to remember the name of the woman staking claim to him, Samantha Simeon, a clingy, overperfumed woman he'd been stuck with most of the night. "I don't understand, Mollie."

She took a bite of ice cream. "I was having lunch with Chloe and Amanda Fortune the day after the ball. They were reading the writeup about it, and I asked to see the picture. There you were. I felt like someone had slugged me in the stomach. I could hardly breathe." She scooped another bit of ice cream into her mouth, her nerves evident. "I said something to Amanda about how I wished someone like you would sweep me off my feet. She ripped the picture out and gave it to me, telling me to wish on it. A month later, you walked into my shop."

Gray hadn't eaten a bite. He set the bowl on the nightstand next to her bouquet.

"I remember thinking at the time," she went on, "that you might be interested if my last name was Fortune."

Stunned speechless, Gray tried to sort out her words. Technically her last name *was* Fortune. He shook his head. Guilt surfaced from deep inside him.

"Oh, it's true," she said, misinterpreting. "Remember the first day you came into the shop, how I maneuvered you out of the workroom and into the open shop?"

"Yes."

"I had to get you past the counter, because this picture was taped there where I could look at it all day and dream about meeting you. Tony recognized you from the picture! Then there's Yarg."

"What about him?"

"Yarg. Gray spelled backward." She set her half-eaten bowl next to his and took his hands. "You saved me."

"From what?" He couldn't believe any of this.

"I had been grieving for my mother. All of sudden you were there to fill up all the sad places of my life. I hadn't dreamed in so long, but I started dreaming again. About you. I went to the library and found every article I could about you. I'm sounding obsessive, I know."

She stopped talking as she seemed to realize the truth of her actions. Gray found he couldn't speak. He never suspected—

"I *was* obsessed," she hurried on, "because for the first time in months I felt alive. I felt like I had something to keep me going. When you walked into my life, a living, breathing dream come true, I almost fainted on the spot." Excitement filled her voice. "Tell me now that we weren't fated to be together."

He'd married someone obsessed with him? Someone who believed he was her salvation or her lifeline or something equally consequential? Being responsible for safekeeping such tenderhearted and naive dreams overwhelmed him. He'd seen himself as her protector almost from the moment they'd met, after never having felt a responsibility toward anyone before. Never. He would have taken care of his mother, had she allowed it instead of marrying James, but he'd never been given that task.

But this revelation from Mollie? Was it some eerie cosmic

connection, as she insisted? Was there more to this relationship than met the eye?

"Say something, Gray."

Guilt piled upon guilt. "I don't think I have the right words."

She squeezed his hands. "Just tell me it doesn't make a difference in how you feel about marrying me. I'm not a stalker or anything."

"Sunshine…" He stopped to gather his thoughts.

A watery sheen made her eyes glitter. She crawled closer and wrapped her arms around him, pressing her cheek to his. "You don't hate me."

He encircled her with his arms. "I don't know what I feel, but it's not hate or dislike or revulsion or any other word that means anything similar. I'm a little flattered, a little in awe, and feeling an enormous responsibility never to disappoint you."

"You've been making my wishes come true, one by one." She angled back a little. "Or did you peek into my birthday-wish box?"

"Is that what that is? I was tempted, but the right to privacy is a big issue with me." He tucked her head under his chin. The flicker of the candles soothed him. "It's been a long, busy day. We should get some sleep."

"I have to rinse out the bowls."

"I'll take care of it."

Mollie had forgotten he was naked. How could she have forgotten that not-so-minor detail? She sneaked a peek at him as he picked up the bowls, then strode out of the room, her gaze following magnetically, attracted to his strong, muscular body. She'd never seen a naked man, live and in person, but she believed he was a prime specimen of the species. With a sigh, she snuggled into the pillow again, awaiting his return. He padded into the room, blew out all but one candle, then crouched beside the bed. She had squeezed her eyes shut.

"It's okay to look," he said, humor lacing the words. "We're fully sanctioned."

She barely opened her eyes. "You're just so beautiful. I didn't expect you to be beautiful."

"And you're perfect." He dragged the sheet from her, caught

the hem of her nightshirt and tugged. "This goes and never comes back."

She sat up as he peeled it off her, her instinct to cover herself overruled by the excitement of his admiring gaze. "Exercising your husbandly rights?"

"Are you objecting?"

"Not me."

He blew out the last candle, then climbed in bed behind her, spooning their bodies, his arm wrapped around her waist, his fingertips grazing the underside of her breast. Unable to stop herself, she wriggled her rear against him and felt him grow hard. An unfamiliar rush of power filled her.

"I'm in control," he said close to her ear. "I know you're not ready."

"I'm throbby, but I could—"

"Not tonight, Sunshine."

The day finally caught up with her. She yawned, closed her eyes and relaxed against him, loving the feel of his body molded to hers, not feeling stifled by it, even though she couldn't move an inch. She drifted for a while, recalling the quiet, lovely wedding in the pretty chapel. For as fast as the event had been put together, it had been truly beautiful and memorable. They even had a videotape of the ceremony tucked away in his briefcase. He'd looked so handsome in his black suit, pristine white shirt and the new gray, black and peach tie she'd purchased to coordinate with her bouquet and his peach rose boutonniere.

"What are you thinking about?" he asked, his voice sleepy.

"The wedding. It was perfect. I felt my mom there with— Oh, no! We didn't call your parents. What if they read about it in the newspaper first?"

"I'll break the news in the morning. The chapel director said we probably had a day's leeway. It's not worth losing sleep over, anyway."

"Easy for you to say. You're not the daughter-in-law." She closed her eyes again. "We need to invite them here to visit."

"They won't come to Minneapolis. Don't take it personally, Sunshine, but they won't ever return. We'll have to be the ones to make the effort."

"I won't give up. They're my family now. It's important that they accept me. Like me."

"Turn around."

She did, then found herself kissed long and hard and well, until her mind emptied of worry. She arched to connect with him, grateful when he lifted her leg over his, bringing them in closer contact. "I'm experiencing a different kind of throb," she murmured, seductively, she hoped. "Now try telling me you can wait until morning."

"Stubborn and persistent," he muttered right before he swept his tongue around her nipple, making it ache.

"In love," she sighed, clamping her hands on his head, encouraging him to linger, making a sound of pleasure when his whole mouth got involved. "And needing to show you how much. Would you mind if I'm on top this time?"

He laughed, low and harsh, like exasperation and surprise mixed together. "Turn on the bedside light and you've got a deal."

"Oh, right. Like you'd really turn me down if I didn't turn on the light." But she leaned across the bed and flipped the switch, then made herself kneel beside him as he studied her. Her heart thumped against her sternum.

"You're so beautiful," he said, pressing a kiss into her palm then laying her hand against his face.

"Compared to others—"

He interrupted her with a shake of his head. "You're the only one, Mollie McGuire. And you'll always be safe with me."

What an odd thing to say, Mollie thought. Safe? From what? But he stopped her thoughts by pulling her down to him, and by the time they fell panting against each other later, she barely remembered the question.

"That's very…nice," Mollie said, trying to muster some enthusiasm for the arrangement her third and final potential employee had put together. Three applicants, three uninspired mixed-bouquet arrangements, three absolute impossibilities. Added to the fact she kept reliving the past twenty-four hours and therefore couldn't concentrate on working, the day amounted to a washout. "I'll call you with my decision," she roused herself to say.

Yarg shrieked his greeting as the woman got to the door. She jumped aside, then glared at Mollie. "This creature has to go, of course." She exited, indignant.

"He's my good-luck charm," Mollie murmured.

"I think he's delightful," a woman said, coming up to the counter. She'd been walking around the store for the past fifteen minutes, openly listening to Mollie's conversation with the leprechaun-hating job applicant, sending Mollie humorously sympathetic looks. She held out her hand. Bracelets jangled, earrings tinkled, a mop of golden curls bobbed. "Tasha Gillette."

"Mollie McGuire." She loved saying her name. "Can I help you with something?"

"I think we can help each other." She pointed to the arrangement. "You're not going to try to sell that perfectly bland thing, are you?"

"I'm going to take it apart and redo it," Mollie said, not hiding her grin. She liked this woman already.

"Move aside, then, and let's see what I can do." She set her backpack under the worktable, grabbed a squattier vase and some hardwood myrtle. "I gather you're looking to hire someone."

Mollie leaned her elbows on the counter and watched Tasha's hands fly as she transferred the Gerbera daisies, alstroemeria, freesia and snapdragons from one vase to the other. "Are you looking for a job?"

"I wasn't. But I just decided that it's exactly what I need." She glanced at Mollie. "You want to hear my life story or just what's pertinent to your thinking about hiring me?"

"Whatever you want to tell me." Mollie already knew she would hire the woman with the wild hair, unsubtle jewelry and peacock-colored jumpsuit.

"I hit the big four-oh last week, and my life is a total cliché. My husband, my *ex*-husband, decided last year to trade me in on a newer, younger model. Enter trophy wife, Angelique, with boobs out there, a haven't-given-birth-yet tummy and an adoring-glances-are-my-specialty personality. My ex is a cardiac surgeon. Classic wife-put-him-through-med-school scenario.'' She spun the vase, stuck in another daisy. "We have twin teenage boys, so baby-sitting's not a problem. I can work weekends, because the boys are enamored of their new stepmommy, who loves to lounge around the pool all day in her bikini, so they spend every weekend there. I'm letting them discover for themselves what a brainless twit she is. I don't have a boyfriend. I don't have to work, because I made sure I got a good lawyer and a great settlement, but I'd like to work *here*. Are you looking for part-time or full-time help?''

"I was thinking part-time, just to give me a break now and then. I've been running this place by myself since my mother died last December.''

"Oh, you poor thing!'' She hurried around the counter to give Mollie a hug, and Mollie's eyes filled instantly with tears at the heartfelt show of sympathy. She wallowed in the comforting embrace for a minute.

Tasha released her, but kept her hands on Mollie's shoulders and looked straight into her eyes. "Tough to be without a mom, huh?''

"Yeah. Never had a dad, either, so there's no history anymore. But I've got Every Bloomin' Thing, and as much as I want to hold on to it, I know I can't do it by myself anymore. If I can find some open space, I'd like to start drying flowers and doing more with them. My baskets are selling really well. I've got to compete with other markets now—even the grocery stores are carrying bouquets. It's so easy to grab a bunch of flowers along with the groceries.'' She straightened the gift cards on the rack next to the cash register. "Plus, my life has changed a little in the past few days and I want some more time.''

"Fell in love, did you?'' Tasha returned to her task. "Just don't give up everything for him, okay? Keep something for yourself.''

"I am. This place.''

"Good. To answer your original question, part-time is okay for now. If I help you grow your business enough, would you consider taking me on full-time?''

"Absolutely. I'd like to build up the wedding-planning end

of the business, as well, but it takes time to go after it. I haven't had the time.''

Tasha wrinkled her nose. ''I'm probably not your gal, then. I'd decorate the church in black crepe and constantly be asking the bride if she was sure she knew what she was doing.''

Mollie laughed. ''I won't ask you to sit in on the planning sessions with the brides.''

''Does that mean I have the job? I don't have a résumé of professional, paid experience, so there's no one to recommend me, but I've served on charity boards and country club committees forever, it seems. Of course, the divorce changed all that.''

''That's terrible! How can they kick you out because—''

''Honey, that's not the way at all. I dumped them. I needed a break from that life, plus I kept running into Angelique. I chaired my last event last month. My friends are envious.'' She lifted the vase, eyed it from all angles, then plunked it on the table. ''I'd charge thirty-two fifty.''

Mollie blinked. Not only had Tasha created a spectacularly original arrangement, she'd nailed the price exactly.

Tasha chuckled. ''I know. I'm good.''

''When can you start?''

''How much are you paying?'' She cupped her breasts, hefted them a little. ''I'm thinking about getting myself a boob job. They've lost their perkiness. That'll cost a little.''

''Don't mess with Mother Nature, Tasha,'' a male voice said.

Mollie spun around upon hearing Gray's voice. He smiled at her, then at Tasha.

''Gray McGuire, as I live and breathe,'' Tasha said. She came around the counter and hugged him.

''You two know each other?'' Mollie asked, amazed and just a little jealous. He should have hugged his wife hello. *He's not a toucher, remember?* And Tasha was the one who instigated the hug.

''Obviously, you do, too,'' Tasha said as she stepped away from him. ''Which is good, because he's about the only recommendation I can offer you, Mollie. He can confirm I was in charge of a charity ball he participated in a month or so ago. Tell her how successful it was, Gray.''

"You're applying for a job?" he asked.

"I've got the job. We were just haggling over the wages."

"I highly recommend her. Tasha also knows Kate Fortune," Gray said. "I'm sure Kate would back her."

"You know Kate?" Tasha asked Mollie. "Proud old bird, isn't she? A helluva woman, that one. I've always wondered what being the matriarch of a family would feel like. A duty? A responsibility? Or a privilege?"

"Kate would probably say yes to all three," Mollie said, "from what little I know of her. I planned a wedding for one of her nephews, who happened to marry my best friend, and I'm doing another Fortune wedding in November."

"Rock and roll, girlfriend! You keep bringing in clients like that, and I'll be taking over your shop completely. Now, offer me a salary I can't refuse."

"Let me consult with my financial adviser." She took Gray by the arm and pulled him around the hutch, out of sight. "I had intended to offer minimum wage, but she's worth more. She'll probably bring in new business by tomorrow afternoon. How much can I afford to pay her?"

"Start her low, promise her quick raises based on increased volume. Offer her bonuses."

"You mean like profit sharing?"

"Exactly. You're going to make more, too, remember. Do you want me to handle the negotiations?"

"I can do it." She took a step away, then came back to him. "I'd like a kiss hello."

He framed her face with his hands and kissed her, a soft and sweet caress that held a lot of promise.

"I've missed you today," she murmured, then she walked away.

Gray admired the gentle sway of her hips. He moseyed around the shop, listening to them argue about salary, then come to an agreement. They were both grinning as they shook hands.

Tasha slung a backpack over her shoulder. At the door she

turned around and pointed a finger at Gray, then at Mollie. "McGuire. Are you related?"

"Just in the legal sense," Gray said, coming to stand beside Mollie.

"No kidding? You're married? I didn't make the connection of your names. You must've tied the knot since the ball, huh? I guess I really am out of the gossip loop." She looked a little sheepishly at Mollie. "Um, you won't take what I said about black crepe seriously, will you? I think marriage is fine—for other people."

"We got married last night," Gray said. "There'll be an announcement in tomorrow's paper."

"Last night? And you're not off on some hedonistic honeymoon, slathering each other with tanning oil?"

"Soon," Gray said, aware of Mollie's full attention to the conversation.

"So, I suppose I have to keep this juicy bit under my hat?" Tasha asked expectantly.

"Seems to me you could kill two birds with one stone, so to speak," Gray replied.

Tasha's eyes lit up. "Pass the news and drum up business. Great idea. Thanks. I'll see you in the morning, Mollie."

The second Tasha was out of sight, Gray pulled a small, gaily wrapped box from his pocket and handed it to Mollie before she could start asking questions. "Happy anniversary."

"Of what?"

"Twenty-four hours ago you agreed to marry me."

Laying her hand on his chest, she smiled. "California time."

"Now who's being logical?"

"You're rubbing off on me."

She moved in on him. Her voice turned sultry. "As soon as I can leave Tasha to run the shop alone, I can rub off on you even more. You could come by at lunchtime and we could go upstairs and—" She purred.

"Let's hope she's a fast learner. Open your present."

She smiled, triumph in her eyes. After tucking the ribbon in her pocket, she lifted the lid. "Oh! Oh, Gray, she's beautiful."

She lifted the tiny fairy pin out of the box. "She looks just like the one on my bell."

"She looks like you." He slipped his hands into his pockets.

"I love it. And I love you." She rose on tiptoe to kiss him. "Thank you. Would you pin it on, please?"

He pinned it on her collar, then smiled at the pleasure in her face.

"Did you talk to your parents?" she asked.

The swift change of subject didn't catch him completely off guard. He'd called her three times during the day, and each time she'd asked the same question. "I did."

"You sound grim."

"It's not you, Sunshine. I didn't follow chain of command, so they are displeased, but it has nothing to do with you. Is that clear?"

"Well, what happens from here? Are we banned from their presence? Will they turn their backs on their grandchildren? My imagination is too fertile."

Let's hope the rest of you isn't. They'd taken a chance last night and this morning by not using birth control. From here on they would. "They intend to throw us a reception, the sooner, the better. Appearances, Mollie."

"I just want the chance for them to know me, know that I'm not a threat to their relationship with you. They should understand I don't want anything to do with your money."

"It's none of their business what our relationship is, financial or otherwise. How long until you close up shop?"

Mollie heard him jangle his keys in his pocket, a sure sign of his retreat from the conversation. Little by little he was opening himself up to her, but all it took was the mere mention of his parents to clam him up again. "I've got an hour to go. Oh, the phone company installed a second line today."

"Good. I'll go upstairs and make the adjustments to your Internet server." He walked away from her.

"Mr. McGuire."

He turned around.

"I need a kiss goodbye."

"I'm just going upstairs."

She waited. After a minute he came back and kissed her, a little too temptingly. She fanned her face when he let her go.

"I'll be waiting," he said.

"I'll hurry."

Eleven

"**Y**ou *what?*" Kelly shrieked louder than Yarg.

"Got married last night," Mollie repeated quietly. She glanced over her shoulder, hoping that Gray would stay upstairs until she finished the phone call. It was ten minutes to closing. He should be getting anxious for her to finish working.

"You got married last night." Disbelief dripped from Kelly's words. "To whom?"

"Gray McGuire."

Dead silence. Mollie found she could smile. If she'd been on the receiving end of the call, she would have lost her ability to speak, too.

"*The* Gray McGuire?"

"Tall, dark and handsome. Brilliant." *Not so lonely, anymore.* "That's the one."

"Why?"

"Why, what?"

"Why so fast? Why so secretive?"

"I love him, Kel. And there wasn't any reason to wait."

"Not even to have your best friend stand up for you?"

"Not even. Be happy for me."

"Oh, I am. I know he can't be after your money, at least."

Mollie laughed. "I want you to meet him. We'll have you and Mac and Annie over for dinner soon."

"His name sure has been mentioned lately at the Fortune family gatherings. Last Sunday, even, at the dinner you missed. I'm not sure it was all positive... Well, I must be mistaken. Gray is respected, right? Known throughout the land. My impression was that he had a black belt in playing the field."

"I think his image is media manufactured. He's really sweet."

"Sweet? I'll have to check this out myself. I'll stop by to-morrow, okay, Mol?"

"I'll be here. Oh, I hired someone today, so maybe we can do lunch occasionally."

"Do lunch?" Kelly laughed. "That's a phrase I haven't heard from you before. Are you already turning California Society—Cripes. Are you moving?"

"He says we're staying here."

"I'll make sure he knows you're not allowed to move. See you tomorrow. I want all the details."

Mollie hung up the phone, locked the door, turned over the Open sign, then hurried upstairs, two steps at a time. Finding Gray huddled over her computer, she wrapped her arms around him and pressed her cheek to his. "I missed you."

He made a sound that might indicate he was aware she was there, but he didn't stop scrolling the screen.

"Is the honeymoon over already, Mr. McGuire?"

He grunted, then typed on the keyboard.

She decided not to be irritated. Instead she straddled him, blocking his view of the monitor. Mission accomplished.

"Is it six already?" he asked, his attention flatteringly complete.

She squirmed in his lap. "More than that, I think," she said, wiggling her eyebrows. "Or it will be soon, I hope."

"And you say you're not good at math."

She flashed him a smile. "What were you working on so intently?"

He unbuttoned the top button of her blouse, then another. "Your P and L." Another. His fingertips grazed her flesh.

"Um. P and L?"

"Profit and loss breakdown for the past three years." He finished unbuttoning her, then slid his hands temptingly around her ribs to unhook her bra with far too much ease.

A black belt in playing the field. "You do that awfully efficiently," Mollie muttered, torn between jealousy and building desire.

"Figure out your P and L?" he asked innocently.

He tugged off her blouse and bra, tossed them aside, then filled his hands with her breasts.

"You're fond of this position, I've noticed," she said, her voice hitching as he thumbed her nipples.

"So are you. Which is why you put yourself here." He bent his head and drew a hard crest into his mouth.

"Perky enough?" she asked, shifting her shoulders, loving the way his hands felt against her breasts, his tongue against her nipple.

He bit down, lightly but arousingly. "You're just right." Honesty rang in his voice. "Everywhere."

"I sure do like this part of marriage," she said on a sigh.

"Are there other parts you don't like?"

"I don't know yet. We haven't done much else." She sucked in a breath as he slid a hand down the placket of her jeans to cup her intimately. "Oh, that's n-nice. Let's go to bed."

He carried her to the bedroom, which she thought was romantic and sexy and brought tears to her eyes. He laid her down, then stretched out on her and kissed her like he'd never kissed her before—and kissing was one of his best skills. *A black belt in playing the field.* No, she wouldn't think about how he'd gotten so good at kissing. And unhooking bras. And making love.

"I'm going to have to leave some protection here if this is going to happen very often," he murmured as he helped to slide off her jeans.

"Are we going to use birth control, after all?" She felt a little awkward being naked while he wasn't. He remedied that right away, however, returning quickly to blanket her body with his again.

"For now. Is that all right with you?"

"We'll talk about it later."

"If you can think *that* clearly, Sunshine, I haven't been doing my job."

"Oh, so now I'm a chore on your to-do list, huh?" It was so important to her that he have fun. She desperately needed to wipe away his somberness. He lived in a world she couldn't begin to comprehend, his head filled with concepts, his heart guarded by barbed wire. Somehow she was going to cut through that wire fortress. And she knew she had to start in the bedroom, the only place he seemed to forget everything else in his structured life.

"How did you know about my to-do list?" He levered himself up enough to look at her. "This is item number fourteen, and I'm behind schedule, so let's speed it up, wife. We should've been done by now and on to item fifteen."

Gray laughed as she poked him in the ribs. He moved his legs to cover hers, keeping her still. "Better be careful how you squirm around or birth control won't be a question at all."

"Oops." She pursed her lips, her eyes sparkling. "What's next on your list?"

"Taking my new bride to our hotel, feeding her dinner, lounging in the whirlpool tub with her, giving her a massage."

"Sounds like one lucky bride." She brushed her fingers through his hair again and again, her smile tender.

He breathed her name, overwhelmed by everything she had come to mean to him in less than a week. "Luckier groom," he murmured right before he kissed her, passionately, infinitely, measuring the progress of her response by her encouraging little moans, the eager arch of her hips, the impatient glide of her hands. Tuned in to her completely, he knew when she started to peak and intentionally slowed her down, dragging out the moment, knowing she was aware of little but pleasure. He wouldn't give in to it himself. Not yet. He needed to take her up again, needed to hear her say she loved him again just as she went over the top, the declaration that no one else had ever made. Did she really love him, though? Or was it infatuation and lust?

And how long would she put up with not hearing the words in return?

Mollie liked seeing her clothes hung next to his in the closet, making the marriage more real to her. His hotel suite was just as she had anticipated—polished wood, elegant upholstery, toe-wriggling carpet. A bathroom bigger than her bedroom at home. A bed that could sleep four. Everything perfectly beautiful and perfectly anonymous.

They'd already eaten dinner, provided by room service. Having finished unpacking the two suitcases of belongings she'd brought along, she returned to the living room, where Gray was busy at the computer. Certain that he wasn't aware of her, she sank to the floor to watch him, something she hadn't been able to do before. She admired the way he could focus so completely—on work, when he needed to, and on her, when he wanted to. She wondered how much time to give him before she dragged him away from that blasted computer.

A knock sounded at the door.

"Do you want me to get that?" she asked.

He turned around, blinked, then stood and moved to the door. "How long have you been sitting there?"

"Half an hour."

His mouth lifted on one side. "You have not."

"Okay. Half a minute."

Chuckling, he disappeared behind a privacy divider to answer the door. After a minute, he came over to where she sat, dropping an envelope in the trash can along the way before he passed her the contents.

"What's this?" she asked.

Somehow he managed not to give her a what-are-you-an-idiot? look.

"It's a credit card, Mollie."

"Dumb question, huh?"

"I want you to use it." He dropped down cross-legged beside

her, not looking anywhere near as comfortable as she did. "Promise you'll splurge a little on yourself."

She smiled at his serious expression. "Okay."

"Promise."

She crossed her heart. "We need to talk about a few things."

"Can we talk on the couch?"

"I've got a better idea." She needed to get him into the bedroom, where he would touch her, not just sit beside her and have a business discussion. "Let's start the water in the bathtub, and while we're waiting for it to fill, we can talk."

Gray detoured into the bathroom and started the tub filling before he sat on the bed, his back against the headboard. He watched Mollie dig out a piece of paper from her purse, then she plopped next to him, angling herself to put her head in his lap. He threaded his fingers through her beautiful hair, fanning it against the deep blue bedspread.

"This is *my* to-do list," she said, fluttering the sheet at him.

"What's on it?"

"Number one, get my name changed on my driver's license, van registration, social security card and everywhere else necessary. Number two, call my mother-in-law."

"You don't have to put yourself through that."

"I knew you were going to say that." She flattened the paper against her stomach. Her eyes pleaded with him. "I'll win her over. I'll call her and write her and visit her. I'll be friendly and caring. She has to love me someday."

Gray marveled at Mollie's innocence, which protected her but also set her up for being hurt, too. "I can see you're determined about this."

"You're very perceptive." She smiled sweetly. "Number three, convince Gray we can't live in a hotel room."

"It's convenient, Mollie. You don't have to cook or clean or do laundry."

"You mean they do your laundry, too?"

"Of cour—"

"Your underwear?"

He stared at her for a minute, then started to laugh. "Everything."

"Well, no one is touching my underwear."

"Except me." He slid his hand inside her blouse and hooked a finger under the edge of her bra, resisting exploring her further. Business first.

"Except you," she said.

"You can't take care of a business, an apartment and this place, Mollie. It would wear you out. Plus, I like living here. My office is here for now. It's quiet."

"Then you can use it as your office all day, but we can live in my apartment at night. We'll redecorate. Get a bigger bed. It'll be nice. You'll see."

Eagerness lit up her face. Not for the first time, he felt the difference in their ages, their experience. Eleven years—but a lifetime. Analytical—emotional. Not much in common, in the end. And yet she balanced him in ways he hadn't considered. Together, they made one well-rounded person.

"Actually, Sunshine, I was thinking we should turn your apartment into your office. You could take your clients there, keep all your business-related files. Now that you'll have help in the shop, you can go upstairs during the day and enter your work into the computer, then you won't have to do paperwork at night like you always have."

"Um, about the computer."

Her tone of voice indicated that this was something he wouldn't want to hear. "What about it?"

"I, um, don't really want to computerize my business."

"Why not?" Did he sound as shocked as he felt?

"It's too much work."

"It's going to save you work."

She sat up. "I order supplies based on instinct and experience. I don't need a tracking program to figure it out for me. It's in my head. And it's easy to write out bills by hand as soon as I'm done with a job."

"Why did you let me install programs and enter your data if you knew you wouldn't use it?"

"Think about it."

He did. He came up blank.

"Gray." She took his hand in hers. "I wanted to spend time with you."

He didn't know whether to be flattered or irritated. "But the P and Ls, and the taxes. You'll need that. I'll tell you what— I'll do the computer work for you."

"You can't do my work and yours. We'd never have time together."

"We'll work it out." He climbed off the bed, intending to turn off the water. "I ordered you a laptop to keep downstairs on the counter."

"It seems like a waste of money when all I'd use it for is e-mailing my husband ten times a day to tell him I love him."

How could he tell her that was worth millions to him when he couldn't even offer her the words in return? He cared about her. He didn't want her to be hurt. He wanted to make her life better, easier than it had been. He wanted to make up for everything her father hadn't given her. Was that love?

Or was that rescuing a damsel in distress?

After turning off the water, he walked back into the bedroom.

"I thought of a compromise," she said. "We can buy a house."

He'd lived in hotels all his adult life. A house meant forever. Responsibility. Time. He couldn't spread himself that thin.

"Soon," he said, then noted her disappointment. "When this business with Knight Star Systems is resolved."

"How long will that be?"

"Not too long."

"Until then, can we at least eat dinner at my apartment before we come back here for the night?"

"Sometimes. Sometimes we can go out."

"And I will do the laundry."

He laughed. "Deal. Now, the water's ready and waiting."

Mollie stood up on the bed, intrigued by how casually he undressed in front of her, wishing she felt that easy. When they were making love, she didn't have much problem with it. And for some reason, after they were done she could sprawl on the bed as if they'd been together forever. She started to unbutton her blouse, forcing herself to relax, but staying on the bed rather than being down on the same level, close to him.

Nervous, she bounced a little as she pulled off her blouse. He'd gotten rid of his shirt and shoes and was unbuckling his belt. He glanced at her at that moment; his hands stilled. She bounced a little higher. Then higher still.

"Care to join me?" she said, using the bed as a trampoline now.

"No, thanks."

"Haven't you ever jumped on a bed? It's fun."

He pulled his belt through the loops and put it aside. "Keep undressing, and maybe I will."

No way. No way could she do that. Her blouse was gone, but that was all. "Come up here with me," she said.

He shook his head.

"I'm not stripping for you."

He grinned, almost irresistibly. Almost. "Then come down here and let me strip you," he said invitingly.

She thought about it a minute, then she bounced to the edge of the bed. "Catch me."

"Don't—"

She launched herself at him. He caught her with a grunt, his arms under her rear, her legs around him, making him stagger a step.

"Idiot. What if I'd dropped—"

She kissed him. Hard. Thoroughly.

"You scared the hell out of me," he said against her mouth, then got distracted by the warm, fragrant skin above her bra. He pulled down one strap, then the other, the cups sliding down her, leaving her exposed. He hefted her a little higher, clamped down on an inviting nipple, then ran his tongue around her tenderly until she moaned. "Coming at me at that speed is like two cars hitting head-on," he said, remembering to make his point.

"You should've joined me on the bed."

He dragged his mouth to the other breast. "I told you I would."

"Only if I stripped."

"Offer's still open."

"That's blackmail."

"Whatever works." He stood her on the bed. "Now or never."

Which is how Gray added two new adventures to his ever-growing list of lifetime learning experiences: bouncing on a bed and making love on the bathroom floor, which is where he finally caught up with his wife when she cheated by jumping off the bed before he'd gotten her underwear off her.

He figured he got the best end of the bargain.

Twelve

Every Bloomin' Thing was jammed with people, thanks to the media's interest and Tasha's telephone chain relaying the hot news. Gray had turned on CNN as they dressed that morning in time to catch the announcement of their marriage as a Top Story, stunning Mollie, then making her laugh. No one had provided the press a photo of her, so only Gray's image had flashed on the screen. The phone started ringing soon after. She was glad to escape, then had found herself inundated with people—she wasn't sure how many were actually customers—the minute the shop opened, including reporters from two national television stations, plus the *StarTribune.*

She called Gray, told him to come deal with the press, then she ordered more flowers from a couple of local distributors to replace what Tasha's friends were buying. Mollie was grateful that they, at least, felt a responsibility to buy something, not just check her out.

Business was starting to settle down when Kelly Fortune arrived at noon with Annie. Gray had maneuvered the press outside and was holding an impromptu news conference in front of several cameras and microphones. Mollie had stood beside him for the first few minutes, squeezing his hand, feeling the comfort of his touch, then returned to her shop with the excuse of too much work to do.

The questions had shifted from their marriage—"Yes, it was sudden, but when something's right, there's no reason to wait"—to a new project having to do with encryption that he was working on. Someone had the nerve to ask if she'd signed a prenuptial agreement, and Gray let them know that their personal life was just that.

Grateful, she'd escaped, afraid those inquisitive reporters would ask her a question about his project, which she couldn't answer. She realized that he rarely discussed his work with her, but he was always busy with it.

"You're royalty," Kelly said, strolling up to the counter, wonder in her eyes.

Mollie reached for Annie, needing to hold on to her, needing something normal and sane to do. Tasha had everything else under control, as if she'd worked there forever, only needing to be taught how to use the cash register.

"It doesn't appear you can 'do lunch' today," Kelly said, looking around.

"As soon as the interest lags, I'll be free. Tasha's a wonder, so maybe in a couple of days I can swing it."

Kelly looked out the window. "He handles the media well."

Mollie heard something in her voice. "But?"

There was a long stretch of silence, then Kelly smiled a little. "Nothing. Nothing at all. He's also even more attractive in person."

"I think so."

"I should've recognized him last week. I don't know why I didn't. Are you happy, Mol?"

Mollie frowned at the sudden change of subject. "Absolutely. Why?"

"You look frazzled."

"So would you, if you'd been inundated by the press and most of the people listed in Tasha's address book. It's been an amazing couple of hours." She pulled Kelly aside a little. Annie stuck her fingers in Mollie's mouth and giggled. "You sweet thing. Let me talk for a minute, okay?" She stared hard at her old friend. "You're not telling me something."

Kelly looked out the window again. "How much do you know about his business dealings?"

"Only what I've read."

"Have you heard him talk about Knight Star Systems?"

Mollie went on full alert. Gray hadn't asked her specifically not to say anything, but she guarded him instinctively. "Why?"

"Some weird stuff has been happening there."

"Weird in what way?"

"I didn't hear the whole conversation between the men on Sunday, so I don't know all the details, but apparently Knight Star has been losing business lately— No. Vendors, I think. Also, Gray's bought a lot of their stock."

"And there's a connection between the two?"

"They were speculating about that possibility."

"Why are any of the Fortunes interested in what happens with Knight Star?"

Annie started to fuss, so Kelly lifted her into her arms and gave her a teething ring. "Stuart Fortune owns it."

Mollie looked away and swallowed. Her mind went blank a minute, then she tried to remember exactly what Gray had said about the company, when she'd asked whether he was going to buy it or take it over. What had he answered? Whatever works? Was that his response?

Don't ask me, Kelly. Don't put me in the middle. She was Mollie's only connection to the past, their shared history a precious and necessary part of her life. But Gray was her husband.

"I wish I could tell you more, Mol. You weren't married to him yet, so their discussion didn't mean much to me, especially since it has nothing to do with Mac or the Fortune Corporation."

"You mean it's not a Fortune company?"

"It's Stuart's baby all the way, the result of a push for something of his own. I don't know much about it, except that he's been in charge of it for twenty-five years or so, along with his duties at Fortune."

Mollie noted the long line forming in front of the cash register.

"I've got to rescue Tasha. Hang around and I'll introduce you to Gray."

"Okay. Although I should be furious that you didn't introduce me the last time I was here." She looked around the shop. "Well, I think I'll do you a favor and *not* buy anything today."

"Ah, the sacrifices a friend will make."

Gray was holding his last one-on-one interview with the press when a black limousine pulled up in front of the shop and Kate Fortune emerged. He didn't know her exact age, but she seemed ageless. He'd danced with her at the ball, had been impressed with her grace. Matriarch was a good role for her, one she performed proudly and well. Another person he was sorry he would hurt. But she'd survived worse, he supposed.

He excused himself from the reporter and made his way to her side as she awaited him.

"Good day, Mrs. Fortune."

"Mr. McGuire." She shook hands with him, her gaze direct. "You're in the news a bit these days. Pulled a fast one, didn't you, getting married without a photographer in sight."

"Kept it secret for twenty-four hours, too," Gray said, leading her into the shop and the shade.

"Quite an accomplishment." She studied his face. "I've had the opportunity to spend a little time with your new bride in recent months. Been popping up at various Fortune events. Always brings sunshine with her."

Gray locked gazes with Mollie as she stood next to a customer who was admiring a display of ceramic frogs. Her smile warmed him. "Yes, she does."

"Hi, Kate!" Tasha waved. "Got myself a job."

"So I see. You'll have to tell me how that happened."

"Kate!" Kelly hurried over and kissed her cheek. Kelly's baby—he couldn't remember her name—turned positively gleeful, pitching herself toward Kate.

"Mind your manners, young lady," Kate said, although her face softened and she took the baby in her arms. "Have you met my grandnephew Mac's wife, Kelly, and their daughter, Annie?" Kate asked Gray.

"We haven't been introduced, no." He shook hands with Kelly.

"We should have been, but Mollie was keeping him to herself."

The woman being discussed wandered up, then slipped her hand into his. "You've met everyone, I see."

"I danced with Mrs. Fortune at the ball. And I remember Kelly."

"Now, don't you all gang up on me," Mollie said, then turned to Kate. "Is there something I can do for you or did you just follow the parade?"

Kate smiled in sympathy. "I was curious to see how you were faring, but I was coming here, anyway. Kelly, you can join the conversation, if you've got the time. In private, if you can find us a spot, please, Mollie."

"We can go upstairs, if you like. Tasha can take care of things for a little while."

Gray watched the women walk away. He smiled to himself. Their ignoring him was exactly what he'd needed to knock him back to earth. The spotlight made him crazy. He turned to rearrange a shelf of knickknacks suffering from too much handling.

"Here. Good practice for you."

Gray turned around. Kate plunked Annie in his arms then strode away. He could see Mollie watching for his reaction and wondered if it had been her idea, but she pointed to Kate as she passed by, then hurried to follow.

"Ever held a baby before?" Tasha asked as he settled the blond beauty in his arms. The shop was strangely empty.

"No." Annie pulled his tie into her mouth and chewed contentedly, her big blue eyes looking right at him. "But I won't drop her."

"I wasn't worried." Tasha moved around the shop, straightening and reshelving. She looked over her shoulder. "Is this uncomfortable for you, my working here?"

"Not at all. Does it bother you?"

"What, because I got stinking drunk and made a pass at you

and you turned me down? I can't imagine why that might embarrass me."

"You weren't yourself that night, Tasha."

"I guess it's a good thing you didn't accept my…invitation."

"Don't give it another thought."

"You were kind to me, Gray. Kinder than I deserved. I was feeling pretty unlovable."

"I didn't turn you down because I wasn't interested." Annie dropped his tie to stick her fingers into his mouth instead. He pulled them out and gave her a stern look. She giggled. "I turned you down," he said to Tasha, "because you didn't know what you were doing."

Her expression said otherwise, but he wanted the conversation to end. He'd met with her twice before the ball to discuss donations for the auction, then at the ball itself. It was only because he'd escaped Samantha Simeon by hiding out in the smoking room that he'd been around at the end of the evening. By then, Tasha had been feeling sorry for herself for too many hours. He'd offered her a ride home, walked her to her door, turned down her offer as gently as possible, and that was the end of it. But he hoped Mollie never found out—for Tasha's sake.

"Well, you could've knocked me over with a look when I discovered you were married to Mollie."

"I'm still a little in shock, myself." He touched noses with Annie, who slapped her hands against his face and promptly gifted him with a raspberry, spattering baby spit all over him.

Tasha handed him a tissue, then patted his arm. "She'll be good for you. Life's too short not to have fun."

Gray smiled at her, then looked up, spotting Mollie, who'd returned and now stood as still as a statue.

"Kate sent me back down. We figured you would have had enough of Annie by now," she said coolly.

He walked to where she waited, scrutinizing him. "She's fine. Aren't you, Annie?" Delighted by the bubble she'd just blown and burst, Annie clapped her hands and blew another one. "But I should get back to work. You can take her."

He passed Annie to her, then bent to kiss Mollie goodbye. She pulled back. Panic jumped two-footed into his soul, bringing a crippling fear that she would leave him, like his father had the only other person who'd loved him.

"Is there a problem?" he asked, already feeling barriers go up, trying not to let them get too high. This was Mollie. The one person he *could* be sure of.

"Should I be jealous of something?"

Her directness threw him. At least he would always know where he stood with her. "No," he said quietly. "Not in the least."

She looked over his shoulder at Tasha, who was greeting a customer. "Am I going to regret hiring her?"

He kissed her then, answering her in a way he thought she would most believe.

"Okay," she whispered. "Okay."

He rubbed his thumb along her cheek. "I have a past, Sunshine. It's not huge or complicated. And it doesn't include Tasha. I won't ever cheat on you. You have my word. I wouldn't risk what we have for anything. "

"I must seem like a baby to you sometimes." She tucked Annie a little closer.

"Mollie, that's the last word I would use. You are all woman to me."

Her eyes expressed her relief. "You'll be back at closing time for dinner, right?"

"Probably earlier than that. Your laptop should be delivered pretty soon. I want to install your Internet server, at least."

She touched his arm as he turned to leave. "I'm sorry I jumped to conclusions."

"Forget it." He saw Annie's eyes flutter shut, her body going limp against Mollie. "I'm not surprised you're such a natural with kids. See you later, Sunshine."

Mollie watched him go, her heart aching. *A black belt in playing the field.* She wished Kelly had never planted the doubt in her mind by using those words. Of course it was harmless with Tasha. Of course. She climbed the stairs to her apartment, wishing she believed the words beyond a shadow of a doubt, wishing she could just trust her instincts. She believed him. Believed in him.

But why had he looked guilty when he'd seen her watching him and Tasha? And there was Knight Star Systems to consider, Stuart Fortune's company. Gray wanted it.

Where was that going to leave her?

Kate Fortune was upstairs in Mollie's apartment, concerned that Mason and Chloe's wedding had hit a snag—a reluctant bride. Mollie was being asked to step in. Kate trusted her, needed her. Would Gray ruin what Mollie was building?

All she could do was ask him.

"What are you doing?" Gray asked, coming up behind Mollie.

She jumped, then flattened her hands over the items spread out on his desk. It was ten o'clock. They'd eaten dinner at her apartment, gone for a walk in the park, then returned to the hotel to do a little work. Everyone in the world, it seemed, had called the California office, wanting an interview. He had to decide what to do about that. Some other newsworthy business was on the horizon, after all.

"You're supposed to be showering," she said, accusation ringing in her words.

"I thought I would convince you to join me."

She hunched over a little more. "Okay. In a minute. I'll meet you."

"What have you got?"

"My old birthday candles."

A few moments of silence passed. "I'll respect your privacy, Mollie." He turned.

"I'll show you." The words came out in a rush, as if she feared she might talk herself out of it, otherwise. She scooped up the candles and dropped them into the box, along with a red pen. Taking his hand, she led the way to the bedroom, then plopped onto the bed.

He sat beside her, waiting. Since she hadn't hesitated much over anything before, he realized exactly how important it was to her. He almost told her to forget it, but the part of him that hungered to know everything about her stopped him.

"Starting when I was five years old," she said, "my mother

had me write down my birthday wish, then she would tape it to one of the candles. For the first couple of years she had to spell the words for me to print, so she knew what they were, but after that it was just me. I've never shared these."

Tell her she doesn't have to. Tell her to keep her secrets. The words shouted at him, appealing to his sense of fair play. He ignored them.

She poked through the candles. "Then on my next birthday I would put a red star on the paper if my wish had come true. Here's the first one, from when I turned five."

"I wish I could go to school," it read. He frowned. "But five is the right age."

"In September, after you turn five," she said. "For two years Mom had been saying, 'When you're five, you can go to school.' Well, my birthday is in April. I expected to go to school that very day."

He pictured her at that age, probably stamping her foot, her red hair in pigtails that bounced.

"It wasn't a pretty sight," she commented drily. "Anyway, I did get to put the star on it later." She pulled out a few more. "Age seven, I wanted a horn for my new bicycle. Not just any ol' horn, either, but one that made an ah-oo-gah sound." She returned that one gently to the box. "Age thirteen, I wished I could 'get those ugly braces off.' By fourteen, I'd really matured. I wished I had a chauffeur to take me to school. I can't even remember why that was so important. Obviously, it never got a red star."

"Do most have stars?"

"Until I met you, eight of them did and ten didn't. Although technically the last one doesn't count." She hesitated, as if realizing she'd said too much, then hurried on. "You've added five stars."

"You're kidding." He peered into the box, curious. "Are you going to tell me which ones?"

"Give me a kiss first."

"Blackmailer," he muttered, but he slipped an arm around her and pulled her close, then kissed the smile right off her mouth.

"My age-eighteen wish," she sighed when he lifted his head. "'I want to be kissed by someone who knows what he's doing.'"

That bit of information pleased him way too much. "What else?"

"When I was ten I wished we could take a trip, anywhere. At eleven I wanted to see the ocean. You made those wishes come true."

The wonder in her eyes humbled him.

"You told me I was beautiful. At nineteen I wished for that."

He brushed her hair back from her face. "I can't believe no one told you that before."

"Well, it's true. And the last red star you gave me was my twenty-first birthday wish. 'I wish I knew what making love feels like.' But now that I know, I can't even describe it. It's different every time."

"For me, too, Sunshine."

"Really?"

He nodded. "Which ones haven't come true yet?"

She shrugged. "Impossible ones. I wanted a baby brother. I wanted a dad."

The warm moment turned icy. That wish should have been granted. It was within Gray's power to do so, to earn himself another red star, but Stuart had made his decision not to acknowledge his daughter. To make Mollie's wish come true would be to cause her more pain. And that Gray would not do.

Mollie wondered about his sudden silence. She closed the lid on her birthday box, without sharing one particular wish, one she still hoped he would make come true, the one that would let her trust him a hundred percent instead of just a little less than that. Then she could share her secret wish with him. A couple of days ago, she thought there was hope. She wasn't as hopeful now, not after what Kelly had told her.

"Can I talk to you about Knight Star Systems?" she asked, climbing off the bed to put away the box. The atmosphere surrounding them changed with her question, getting cooler, quieter.

"What about it?"

"Is it true that Stuart Fortune owns it, but it's not a Fortune Corporation entity?"

"Yes. I don't know why Stuart didn't put it under the Fortune umbrella, but that's the case. It's publicly held, though."

"And you said you're going to either buy it or take it over, right?"

"Yes."

"Have you approached him about buying it?"

"Not yet."

She stood a distance from him, an invisible barrier between them. "I don't know much about takeovers except that 'hostile' usually precedes it."

"Not always, particularly not if the company isn't performing well. The stockholders have to believe the business isn't being run well in order for them to go along with a takeover. That would mean the shareholders got substantially lower or no dividends for a few quarters, or the stock value is plummeting. It's all financially motivated, whether or not it's hostile."

"And that's not the case with Knight Star?"

He hesitated. "Not in the past."

"But now it is?"

"Yes. Somewhat."

"Have you had anything to do with that, Gray?"

His hesitation made her heart turn over.

"What have you heard?"

She looked directly at him, irritated by his evasiveness, knowing how uncomfortable he was by the way he jammed his fists in his pockets. She wanted him to volunteer the information, to come clean. "My best friend married a Fortune. And I'm counting on Chloe Fortune's wedding to showcase my abilities as a wedding planner. But on top of that, I've been invited to their homes, taken to lunch. Trusted. I care about them as friends, plus I'm working hard at growing my business, as you call it. You can't swoop in and destroy that. And don't you dare tell me I don't need to work. My work ethic is as strong as yours, even if my profits seem like a grain of sand compared to your beach."

"Mollie—"

Her eyes filled with tears. She hated that. She'd wanted this to be a straightforward, business discussion. "Don't put me in the middle, Gray. I'd choose you, because my loyalty will always be to you first, as yours should be to me. Haven't you got enough in your life without Knight Star Systems?"

"No."

She didn't know this side of him, this rigid businessman. "I'm begging you. Please don't do this. I'll lose everything except you."

"And I'm not enough?" Gray pushed himself off the bed and walked up to her, furious at himself. He might as well be twirling his mustache. Just how low could he sink? He cupped her shoulder. "Ignore that. You caught me off guard. Nothing is final yet, Mollie."

"But you resigned as CEO to move here and take over this company."

"I have plans I haven't told you about."

"Why haven't you?"

"There just hasn't been time."

She frowned. "That's really lame."

He ran a hand through his hair, buying himself a couple of seconds. "I suppose it is. I promise I'll give you all the details." Except he wouldn't tell her about her father. That secret he would guard with his life.

"Now. I want to know what your plans are for Knight Star Systems."

He crossed his arms. "Knight Star is a security company that's already highly successful. I want to expand it into *the* high-tech leader of security programs. And most of all I'm going to make computers safe. I've been working on encryption software that I think will change everything, keeping us free from hackers and other people who steal our identities and make our lives hell."

"Can't you do that on your own, without Knight Star?"

"Of course. But I want the company. It's important to the whole package." He could see he hadn't convinced her, but there wasn't any more he could tell her, either. "Still care to join me in the shower?"

"I don't think so."

The punishment should fit the crime, Mollie. This doesn't. He retreated. Her attitude toward him had changed now that other people were intruding into their life. Would she be swayed, then, by others' opinions, or would she let him prove himself?

Mollie waited until the shower water was running before she moved. Such a complicated man she'd married. She loved him. That hadn't changed. But she didn't like him much at the moment.

She didn't care what he said, she was wearing her nightgown tonight. She needed that distance. Hurrying to undress, she slipped the gown over her head before she hung up her clothes, not risking his catching her naked and changing her mind. He was good at that.

Unclasping her watch, she opened a nightstand to put it away. She started to close the drawer when something caught her eye. A Popsicle stick?

Mollie lifted it out. Two thirds of the stick was stained red. A date was written on it—the night they'd had the Thai food for dinner. He could only have the stick if he'd taken it from her trash.

He'd taken it. Kept it. Treasured it.

Her throat burned; her eyes welled. He did love her. Or something as close to love as he was capable of. He wouldn't take over that company and ruin her friendship with the Fortunes. He wouldn't hurt her like that. Maybe he didn't know it yet, but she did.

She tucked the stick back in the drawer, took out her watch and put it on the nightstand itself, stripped off her nightshirt and hurried into the bathroom. She saw him reach for the handles as if to turn off the water just as she got there.

Yanking open the door, she thought she caught a look of surprise on his face, but her vision was a little blurry. She wrapped her arms around him, squeezed him tight. He held her in return, his cheek resting against her hair.

"I love you so much," she said with conviction.

"Sunshine..."

"Just promise me that if you go ahead with this deal, you'll tell me. I need to be prepared. I won't break your confidence, but I don't want to seem like the ignorant little wife."

"I promise."

She tipped her head back, needing his kiss, needing his strength. Some people would probably call her foolish, but she believed in him. He may have started as her fantasy, but she knew he was all too human. And she figured she could forgive him just about anything.

Thirteen

Mollie studied Mason Chandler and Chloe Fortune, seated on the couch in her not-yet-turned-into-an-office living room. Mollie had called Chloe right after Kate Fortune left her apartment last week. "She seems too apprehensive for a bride," Kate had said, her concern probably understated. Kate wasn't the type to make something out of nothing. And, in typical Kate fashion, she'd offered her assistance should Chloe drop the ball completely. The wedding would be the fairy tale come to life, with or without Chloe's input.

Uncomfortable with that notion, Mollie hadn't pushed Chloe, so almost a week passed before Chloe scheduled an appointment, but they'd accomplished little so far. Mollie repeated questions to Mason, who sat, stood and paced repeatedly, obviously not focused on the wedding plans.

On top of that, Chloe wouldn't—or couldn't—make decisions on even the most trivial matters. She waved a hand, told Mollie to choose, then turned her gaze on Mason again, her expression vacillating between concern and longing. Mason ignored her.

Ignored Mollie. Ignored everything. Mollie wondered why he'd bothered to come.

"Your dress is in," Mollie said to Chloe. "You need to schedule a fitting with the seamstress."

"I will."

"Soon, Chloe." She passed her a piece of paper. "Your bridesmaids need to be fitted, as well."

"I'll tell them."

"I can take care of it, if you'd prefer."

"No, I'll do it." Her gaze followed Mason as he paced along the window again. "It's all so complicated."

"That's why you have me," Mollie said, infusing cheerfulness into her voice, although she wondered whether Chloe thought it was the wedding or Mason that was so complicated. "I do the research, the phone calls and the negotiations. All you do is make the final choice."

"Maybe we should just elope, if this is all too much for you," Mason said to Chloe.

Well, at least he was listening to the conversation, Mollie thought, relieved, even if she thought she could hear sarcasm in his voice. Then she realized she wouldn't get to complete the job. "But—"

"I can't elope," Chloe said after a glance at Mollie. "My family would never forgive me."

"It seems simpler, that's all. I don't like how this is getting to you." He turned to Mollie. "You eloped. What do you think?"

"I didn't have family to worry about."

He scrutinized her. Something about him made her nervous, as if he could see into her soul. It was positively eerie.

"You didn't know McGuire for long."

"No."

"Are you regretting it?"

"Mase!" Chloe turned to Mollie. "I'm so sorry. He has no right—"

Mollie cut her off with a gesture. "Absolutely not. I don't regret it at all." She challenged him with her eyes.

His all-seeing gaze made her quiver inside. This was a man

who seemed to know what made people tick, so why couldn't he see that Chloe wasn't overwhelmed by the impending wedding, but nervous about it? Or was it that she was nervous about who she was marrying? Mollie thought she herself would be petrified of him. Gray was complex but he wasn't scary.

"I think we should go now," Chloe said, pulling her purse strap over her shoulder as she stood. "I'll call you soon, Mollie. We'll talk again."

"That'll be fine."

Chloe started down the stairs. Mason stopped next to Mollie and leaned close. "If you ever need anything, call me."

Her heart thumped. "What could I possibly need that my husband can't provide?"

"Being young doesn't mean being foolish. I know you're no fool, Mollie. The public spotlight can turn a person into charcoal. If you need a break from it, let me know."

"I'm sure that won't be necessary, but thank you."

"Mase!"

He cupped Mollie's shoulder, squeezing a little as he passed by. She sank onto the sofa the minute he was out of sight. Innuendo. Rumors. Gossip. She'd heard it all in the past week.

She wished Gray were home. He'd been in California for three days, and she hated sleeping alone. She'd stayed in her apartment each night, although Tasha had invited her over for dinner once and she'd had a wonderful time.

But she wanted Gray with her. The longer he stayed away, the better the chance that his father could convince him not to resign. Mollie didn't want to move there, although if it meant his not taking over Stuart Fortune's company, she could live with that. She would lose the Fortunes as friends either way. She would rather lose them because she had to move.

She should have gone with him, taken the opportunity to spend time with his mother—except that Tasha wasn't ready to handle the shop alone yet, not for whole days. Plus business had almost doubled, which meant a whole new game plan for the shop if the trend continued. She didn't know how long she could count on her new celebrity status and Tasha's friends' curiosity to hold strong.

Feeling melancholy, she opened her computer, then typed an e-mail. From MollieM: "I MISS YOU!!!!" She typed the message in all capital letters because he'd told her it was the equivalent of shouting. He responded almost instantly.

From GKMcGuire: "Is something wrong, Sunshine?"

From MollieM: "No. Can you call me?"

From GKMcGuire: "Not right now. They think I'm looking up some data. I feel like a kid caught sending notes in class. I'll call when I'm free. Are you sure you're okay?"

From MollieM: "A husband should be with his wife." She typed a happy-face icon, then hit the Send key.

When Gray retreated to his office after the meeting, he brought up Mollie's last e-mail. He smiled—not at the happy face—but at her words. "A husband should be with his wife," not "A wife should be with her husband." No "whither thou goest" for *his* wife. He'd needed her with him these past few days, but he was also glad she hadn't been subjected to the first real anger he'd ever seen from his parents. Apparently they knew better than he what he wanted out of life.

He wasn't eighteen anymore. He'd navigated the business world, the social world, the *real* world. He didn't need a mentor. And, no, he didn't need a psychiatrist, either, he'd told his mother when she'd offered up that idea. He hadn't realized how much they expected of him, how much they took for granted. They had seemed to encourage his independence, but it was all a lie. They'd actually plotted every step of his life. Well, almost every step. Or perhaps they'd interfered in his personal life more than he'd thought.

Which didn't matter now. He had Mollie. She was his wife. His parents couldn't change that.

He picked up the telephone and dialed, turning in his chair to look out the window as the phone rang.

"Every Bloomin' Thing, Mollie McGuire speaking."

"So, have you made a mistake and said Mollie Shaw in the past ten days?" he asked. He could almost feel her warmth seep through the phone lines.

"Not once. Are you on your way home?"

"Tomorrow. My mother said you called."

She sighed. "An exercise in futility."

"Remember that they're upset with me, not you. It'll take some time. I'm not sure *I'll* be on speaking terms with them when this is over."

"I'm not giving up. She told me in the garden at her house that you were everything to her."

"She did?"

"It's the truth. Do you think they would ignore grandchildren?"

Gray sat up straighter. "Are you trying to tell me something?"

She laughed, a warm, sweet sound. "I think it would be too soon to tell."

"We've been careful. Since the first couple of days."

"And one other time," she said, reminding him of the lunch that hadn't included a meal the day before he left for California. "As I said before, I'll go on the Pill if that eases your mind."

"Okay," he said. "Schedule an appointment."

"I already did."

"I hear that smile of yours, Sunshine. You only seem docile. You're not in the least."

"Would you be interested in an obedient, submissive wife?"

"I believe sometimes I would."

She laughed, as he'd intended. "Well, then, sometimes I will be. Just catch me on the right day."

"The twelfth of never?"

"I love you."

The words still blindsided him. He wished he could return them as easily, but they stuck in his throat.

"Call me later," she said, filling up the empty space.

"I will. Don't tell Tasha all our secrets, okay?"

"Are you kidding? Our life is totally tame compared to hers. She'd be bored to tears."

Which meant that Mollie guarded their privacy as much as he did. He was grateful. "Goodbye, my Sunshine."

"Goodbye, my heart."

He waited for her to hang up, then he set the receiver in the cradle without disturbing the air where her tender words still drifted. He didn't know what he'd done to deserve her. He had intended to use her as a tool to get his own justice. It would have destroyed her.

He would even the score with Stuart Fortune—Knight Star belonged to Gray—but Stuart's family wouldn't suffer the same humiliation that Gray and his mother had. No eye for an eye, but a business deal, and a slice into Stuart's ego, then the return of the company into the proper hands. Stuart would still have his position at Fortune Corporation. His life would continue, if a little fractured.

The victory wouldn't be as complete, but Gray could live with winning the battle, if not the war. There was Mollie to consider. And Mollie mattered most.

"It's a surprise," Mollie said as Gray drove according to her directions out of the city and into the countryside.

"A surprise. It's nine o'clock at night on a Tuesday—a work night—and you want to go for a drive in the country."

"That's right." She wished for something other than bucket seats. Wished she could scoot over beside him. He'd been so stressed for the past month. At first the news of his resignation from McGuire Enterprises was a closely guarded secret. Then once the news was made public, he'd been inundated with more media attention than after their wedding, and it hadn't let up. She wanted him to have one peaceful evening, so she'd fixed him dinner at her apartment, which was now mostly her office, then had given him a back rub. When they climbed into the car to go to the hotel, she instructed him otherwise.

"You know I don't like surprises, Mollie."

"We need to work on changing that."

She thought he sighed, but she knew he wasn't perturbed or merely humoring her. She had succeeded in her goal. He was learning to have fun. His life was in chaos, but he could laugh about it. She figured he was ready for this surprise. "Okay, pull over here. You can park right between those trees, facing the lake."

He jammed on the brakes. "Oh, no, you don't. I can see what

you're up to." A car honked, forcing him to ease into the spot she'd pointed out. "We are not staying. We have a perfectly good bedroom. I'm well past the age of necking in a car."

"That old, huh?" She turned off the ignition and yanked out the keys, then dropped them down her dress.

He slammed his palms against the steering wheel. She was pretty sure he was laughing. He held out a hand but didn't look at her.

"Give me the keys, Mollie. I'm a well-known and respected businessman. We're married, for God's sake! I am not going to get caught necking with my wife."

"You need to be able to cross this off your lifetime to-do list."

"Like hell I do."

"Front seat or back?" she asked cheerfully.

"Give me the keys."

"Get them yourself."

Gray heard the dare in her voice. "I'll get them, and we won't be staying here afterward."

"Give it your best shot."

He didn't laugh. He wanted to, though. Eyeing the low neck of her dress, he planned his strategy. She kept one fist pressed between her breasts, undoubtedly against the keys nestled in her bra. He could distract her with kisses, which always worked. Some things were predictable about her.

"I'm waiting," she taunted.

He leaned toward her.

"Gonna divert my attention with kisses, huh? Good idea. That way we won't be 'necking in the car.'"

"You've got this all figured out."

"I believe I do."

He angled toward her a little more, then ran his finger along her low neckline, dipping his finger a little farther beneath the fabric with each pass—and not encountering any other fabric. "You're not wearing a bra."

"Nope."

"Which means the keys aren't...are—"

"Elsewhere."

He molded his hand over her warm, firm breast, and felt her push toward him a little. She dropped the fist she'd used as a decoy, giving him better access.

"You're not playing fair," he said, moving his hand to the other side.

"This is a game—" her breath caught "—where you make up the rules as you go."

He pressed his lips right below her ear, tasted her fragrant skin. "So are you naked under that dress?"

"Find out for yourself." She turned her head, aligning their mouths. He groaned as hers opened, welcoming him, then he slid a hand under her skirt, along her thigh.

"We're steaming up the windows," he said.

"You're fast."

"Mollie." His fingers touched the silky triangle of her femininity and then metal. He scraped the keys out onto the floorboard, then put his hand back, loving the damp warmth he encountered, devouring her mouth with his at the same time. His body was contorted over the console; she was holding herself at an odd angle. "When did you get rid of your bra and underwear?"

"Before we left the apartment." With her tongue, she drew a hot, moist trail down his neck. Her hand came down to blanket him, tease him. "I was really offended that you didn't notice," she breathed. "I'm not *that* small."

"I was anticipating getting home and getting you into bed." He used his fingers on her until she lifted her hips high. "I can't believe I'm doing this," he muttered as he moved his thumb in a slow circle. She was moments away from climax. Moments—

Light streamed into the car. Gray took a second to look Mollie over. Clothes in place. All important body parts covered. Then with a sigh he snatched the keys from the floorboard, turned the ignition on far enough to activate the power switches, then rolled down his window. "Officer," he said, wincing as the light hit his eyes.

"Aren't you a little old for this, sir?"

"Dougie?" Mollie's voice held surprise and laughter. She crouched low. "Is that you?"

The officer shifted the light. "Mollie? Damn it, what are you doing up here?"

"Necking with my husband. He never got to as a teenager. I felt his education needed completing."

Gray wanted to sink under the steering column. Unlike Mollie, he didn't find the situation amusing.

"You want me to send out a call to leave you alone?" the big, uniformed man asked.

"No, we do not," Gray said, sending a look Mollie's direction.

"I think we're going home," she said meekly. "Good to see you, Dougie."

"You, too, Mollie. Nice to meet you, sir."

He whistled as he walked away. Gray was stuck because the police car blocked his path. The second it pulled away, Gray was on the road.

"Gray—"

"Not a word."

"But—"

"I mean it."

Silence surrounded them all the way to the hotel and up the elevator. She matched him stride for stride as they walked down the short hallway to their suite. He rammed the keycard in the door, then let her go ahead of him. When the door shut behind them, he grabbed her hand and walked into the bedroom.

And then he kissed her, with gratitude for the adventure she'd brought to his life, with anticipation of everything she would bring to his future.

"You're not mad at me?" she asked as he stripped off her dress, leaving her beautifully naked. Temptingly naked.

He yanked off his own clothes, then he moved her to the bed, following her down. A heartbeat later he was inside her. "I should be," he murmured, angling down to suck a hard nipple into his mouth. "I damn well should be."

"But?"

He moved inside her. "You were right. It was dangerous." He pulled back. "Exciting. I don't know how far I would've gone if the cop hadn't come along." She moaned, arched, dug her fingers into his buttocks. He plunged, retreated, plunged again. "Is this what you want?"

She made sounds of acquiescence.

"Then take it all, Mollie. Take it all." He could feel her doing exactly that, surrounding him, holding him deep inside, then convulsing around him, her whole body reacting, climbing, arching, soaring. When she slowed the rhythm he urged her to try again. "Don't relax. Don't let yourself come all the way down. Let yourself fly. I want you to."

He heard her say his name, heard her say she loved him, triggering an explosion inside him, not physical release, but emotional. Life. Hope. Happiness. It filled him, overflowed from him, imprisoned him. He pulled her leg higher along his hip so that he could get closer. Impossibly closer.

"Are you with me?" he asked.

Mollie managed to tell him yes. He wasn't hurting her—he could never hurt her—but he dominated. Controlled. Pleased. "Why are you doing this?" she asked, as she responded again, shocked by how much she loved this side of him, knowing somehow she'd caused it—which filled her with power and satisfaction.

"Because I need you." He kissed her violently. "I need you."

Her world blasted apart with his words. It was more than a beginning. It was a huge, huge step for him. Love poured out of her as he groaned the words again, at the same moment following her into the explosion of light and sound that got brighter and louder every time they made love. He grabbed her to him, his body going stiff and still, his chest vibrating with sound, then he collapsed on her, holding her as if she would disappear, when nothing could be further from the truth.

Mollie came slowly aware of his weight against her, of his face burrowed against her neck. Floating on her memories, she brushed his hair with her hands, again and again, until he relaxed, rolling to his side and pulling her along. Their legs entwined. She leaned back just far enough to see his face. "We're going to have a baby," she said into the peacefulness.

Gray felt his heart stop. *What? What had she said?* "We're having a baby?"

She nodded. "I've known for six hours. It was the hardest secret I've ever kept. I had intended to tell you at the lake. I figured that would make everything really memorable."

"This whole evening is written in indelible ink in my mind." He could see expectation in her eyes. How could he tell her how he felt when he couldn't put it into words himself? Every protective instinct doubled. Nothing and no one would hurt her or their child. He brushed her hair from her face and kissed her gently. "I thought you were going on the Pill."

"I was supposed to start them when my period came. It never came, so I went back to the doctor today. We pretty much figured out when I conceived."

"When? We were careful after the first couple of days."

"Remember the second time you came home from California. The last time, when everything was settled and the announcement made?"

He smiled at the memory. "Oh."

"Which means I'm about four weeks along. Are you okay with this? I know it's sooner than you wanted."

"I didn't do much to prevent it, did I? I must have wanted it as much as you. How do you feel?"

"Happy. Fine. My breasts are a little tender."

God. He'd been rough with her. Made her climax twice. Would that hurt the baby?

"Are you happy?" she asked.

"Yes." He stroked her back, his hands shaking a little. He had to call the doctor, swallow his embarrassment and ask if he could have hurt the baby. "I'll take good care of you, Mollie. I swear."

"Well, of course you will. We'll take good care of each other." She pressed a kiss to his chest. "Now, let's call your parents."

He knew he didn't stand a chance of talking her out of it, so he dragged the phone onto the bed and dialed. After he shared the good news, he passed the phone to Mollie, then rubbed her back as she talked and smiled and laughed.

"She sounded emotional," Mollie said after she hung up. She curled like a kitten against him, enjoying the massage he hadn't stopped giving her.

"Do you think so?"

"I know so. There was a little catch in her voice. And she was very concerned that I take good care of myself."

"Is that when you told her that I would take very good care of you, too?"

"Mmm-hmm."

"Just when I think she won't surprise me."

"I told you there was hope."

He kissed the top of her head. "I remember, Sunshine."

"Grandchildren are second chances."

Gray considered that. Would his mother try to make up for all that had gone wrong before?

"I'm so happy," Mollie whispered, then her body relaxed against him completely.

A terrible sense of dread came over him, unnamed but real. Within touching distance. Happiness never lasted long.

He pulled up the blankets and wrapped his precious wife close to him, a barrier against whatever threat hovered. His fear didn't fade. His heart thundered with it. Then he lay awake all night, keeping it at bay. Keeping her safe.

Fourteen

Mollie picked up a black teddy in the Sheer Pleasure lingerie shop and examined it critically. Gray had not made love to her in a week, ever since he'd found out she was pregnant. She wasn't putting up with it for one more night. In her van was a bouquet of carnations—his favorites—and a lamb's wool duster she intended to sweep along his entire body. The image made her smile. He'd thought she was a hard woman to resist before. Wait until he walked into the scene she was setting.

She returned the black teddy to the rack and selected a rich, royal blue one, a little lacier than the black, definitely a change of pace from the unimaginative stuff she'd never gotten around to replacing. He would be pleased that she would finally use her credit card, too. He'd been after her about that. "Splurge a little," he told her repeatedly. Well, she just might invest in a few more sexy garments while she was in the mood.

"Mollie?"

Mollie stifled a groan. The very first time she tries to do something sexy, she gets caught. And by Marie Fortune, Stuart's wife.

The sixtyish woman offered the slightest of smiles. "I thought that was you," Marie said. "Still on your honeymoon, I see."

"Hi. Just taking your advice."

"Mine? What would that be?"

"At Kelly's baby shower, you gave her lingerie, remember?" Mollie asked. She was so uncomfortable around Marie, knowing what she knew about Stuart. And Gray. And Knight Star Systems.

"I remember."

"You also said something about us young girls today, how we don't know how to keep a husband interested."

Marie did smile then. "I recall that now. Someone asked if that was how I kept Stuart from straying."

"You said you'd murder him if he tried."

"And he's still quite alive." Marie fingered the blue teddy. "This should go a long way toward keeping your new husband interested."

"I keep wondering if I should go with black. Or red."

"Try this little test, why don't you. Right before you go to sleep tonight, ask him what color the teddy was." She tucked her purse close to her side. "You look very happy, Mollie."

"Oh, I am. I love my husband, and we're going to have a baby."

"Are you? How exciting for you. Well, better take advantage of that little bit of lace while you can." She studied Mollie a few seconds. "It was nice seeing you."

"Thanks. You, too." Mollie shivered. That woman made her so nervous.

Armed with her tools of seduction, she headed for the hotel suite a half hour later. She was tired of him treating her like glass. His fears were just that, and she intended to annihilate them tonight.

Gray curved his hand over the telephone after he hung up, wondering whether he should be glad he'd returned from his meeting early. Stuart Fortune had just called from the hotel lobby. He wanted to meet with Gray. Now.

He glanced at the clock. Mollie wasn't due home for at least two hours. Time enough to have a face-off with Stuart and deal with the aftermath.

The knock was strong, sharp. Authoritative. Gray took easy strides across the living room, around the privacy wall, then opened the front door. Like the rest of the family, Stuart Fortune wore power well. He was dressed in a custom-tailored, immaculate suit that emphasized the tall, broad-shouldered frame he'd passed on genetically to his sons, Jack and Garrett. But there was a certain aura all his own, too. One of a man comfortable with who and what he was.

"Come in," Gray said, not offering his hand, not expecting Stuart to offer his. He led the way into the living room.

"You're sure your wife won't interrupt us?" Stuart asked, sitting in a wing chair.

"She'll be at the shop until six. If she's going to be early, she'll call." Gray remained standing.

"We've never had a conversation, but I've had the occasion to observe her recently. She's a nice young woman. Full of life."

"Her mother did a good job raising her," Gray said, appalled at Stuart's nerve, at the utter disconnection from Mollie as his own flesh and blood. "Shall we get down to business?"

"I would appreciate it if you would sit down, Mr. McGuire. If not, I'll stand. I don't believe this needs to be confrontational."

Gray sat, tasting victory.

"A few months back I was made aware that you'd been buying stock in Knight Star Systems," Stuart said. "And now you've amassed the largest number of shares owned by an individual other than myself."

"Yes."

"I bought Knight Star twenty-five years ago. Since then it's shown a steady rise in orders and profits."

"You maneuvered a takeover of Knight Star twenty-five years ago, Mr. Fortune, not a buyout."

Stuart shifted slightly. "Of course. Which doesn't negate the success of the business. Until recently."

Gray waited.

"As the second-largest shareholder, you might be interested in knowing that the business has taken a few hits lately."

"What kinds of hits?"

"Vendors suddenly can't manufacture the components we need to produce the security systems. Repair parts aren't available when a piece of equipment breaks down in our factory. Orders are canceled for no good reason. Projects are underbid by large percentages. Profits are in decline."

"What do you intend to do about it?"

"I should be asking you that question—as the source of the problem."

Gray smiled slightly. "Am I?"

Stuart leaned forward. "One of the people you contacted happens to be an old friend of mine. He told me you offered him a better deal than I was giving him if he'd sell his chips exclusively to McGuire Enterprises. When I put some of my other vendors on the spot, they finally admitted similar circumstances."

"Nothing illegal in that."

"No. It's business. However, it's taking profits out of your pocket, since you stand to lose almost as much as I. What's really baffling is that you resigned at McGuire Enterprises. So, increasing their profits at the expense of mine—and yours— confuses me. I can only deduce, then, that this is personal. You're out to ruin me." His gaze never wavered. "In the meantime you're going to force people into unemployment. I need to lay off twenty percent of my workforce. They know it. Are waiting for the pink slips to be handed out, even though I've always promised them job security. Morale is extremely low. I don't understand why you're doing this. I've never heard a negative word about you. You're a tough, sound, fair businessman." He made a gesture of bewilderment. "Enlighten me, please."

The moment of truth. Gray had waited so long that he almost couldn't speak. "My father died when I was eight," he said at last. "My mother remarried, and her husband adopted me. My birth name is Knight. Grayson Knight." There. He'd said his name out loud for the first time in twenty-five years. He had thought it would feel good. But it only felt different.

Stuart blinked. Stared. He dragged a hand down his face, then his body sagged. "Charlie Knight was your father."

"Yes."

"I guess I've been waiting for you to show up someday."

"Have you?"

Stuart rose from the chair and moved to the fireplace. He leaned his palms against the mantel. "I've lived with the consequences of what I did. If you think I haven't suffered, you're wrong."

"Small payment for the death of a good, kind, happy-go-lucky man, who loved that company and its people. Who loved his family." Gray approached him. "He was my father. You destroyed him. I want you to know what that feels like."

"What do you intend to do?"

"I want Knight Star. It's my inheritance."

Stuart shook his head. "I won't give it up. I made a promise after your father died. I would make that company the best of its kind. I would treat the employees fairly. We would be a family. They would never be in danger of losing their jobs. I didn't even shelter the business under the Fortune Corporation because I wanted to be sure that no one would make decisions except me. I've changed. I'm not the power-hungry man I was. Ask anyone."

"Oh, you're universally admired," Gray said. "As are all the Fortunes. Reigning royalty."

"I'd say you've created a fine kingdom for yourself, as well." He straightened his spine. "You think you can convince the rest of the shareholders that I can't run this business responsibly and profitably. I'm here to tell you, they won't give up on me that easily."

"They gave up on my father. If *you* could convince them, there's no reason why *I* can't."

Stuart was silent a long minute. Then he sighed. "You obviously don't know what really happened. No one wanted to give up on your father. He made a mess of the company finances, and he borrowed against his shares, putting the company in further danger of bankruptcy. Not to mention that he was headed for personal bankruptcy, as well."

Gray's lifelong beliefs twisted into a tight, painful knot. His mother had refused to speak of what had happened. The public details of the takeover were sparse, but specific, with no mention of bankruptcy. He'd read every newspaper article written about it. Maybe what hadn't been written in the articles was what mattered, not what *was* there.

Gunnar Swensen had filled in the blanks for Gray. Although demoted soon after the takeover, Gunnar was head accountant during the transition of power. He knew that Stuart Fortune had paid off Mollie's mother, had proof to that effect, having cut a check to her out of company funds, but recorded as a loan to Stuart. The paperwork Gray had in his possession proved Karen had been paid a substantial amount of money. And the resentful Gunnar had made it his business to know who the very-married Stuart Fortune was having an affair with. Information was power.

"My father was a good man," Gray said, hearing the defensiveness in his voice, wishing his emotions weren't so involved. He reached for the cool neutrality that was usually there for him to grab, but he couldn't find it. He'd changed. Because of Mollie.

"Charlie Knight was one of the most likable people on earth," Stuart said. "But he was an incompetent businessman. He took too many risks. Foolish risks. I'm sorry if I'm telling you something you didn't know, but you need to hear the truth before you destroy something good. Your father gambled. And he lost. We did whitewash a lot of the details for the press, so that you and your mother wouldn't suffer so much."

"I don't believe you." *You've lied about other things.*

"Some community leaders came to me, afraid the business would fold. It was at a time in my life when I had something to prove—to myself and my family. I'd ridden on the Fortune coattails for too long. I was at that critical midlife point of crisis in almost every man's life, and I rebelled. Perhaps you can understand that. I don't know why you resigned from McGuire Enterprises, but perhaps you're looking for validation of your own abilities, your own worth, as I was."

The accuracy of Stuart's words stung, but Gray focused on

the most important issue. "You're saying my father had already destroyed the company?"

"Yes. I'm sorry, but yes. I've tried to make amends for the way I handled everything in the beginning. I made mistakes." He came up to Gray. "You're young. When you're my age will you be able to look back without regrets? I know I would regret not fighting you for Knight Star. I've learned that much about myself. I won't give it up."

Gray raked his fingers through his hair. What was he to believe? His memories—or the man who'd stolen his father's company, who'd taken his livelihood away, leaving him a failure. "If you've changed, if you've really become a better man, why haven't you acknowledged your daughter?"

Silence fell like a velvet theater curtain, bringing a stunning, deafening absence of sound.

"My what?" Stuart asked, his voice a mere rasp.

"Mollie. Your daughter."

Stuart shook his head. Blinked his eyes. "Your wife?"

"The way you took over my father's company is nothing compared to how you've treated her." He listed Stuart's crimes. "You ignored her all these years. Lived in that grand home, while she shared a tiny apartment with her mother. Gave your sons everything, while she had so little. You've been idolized by the community, placed on a pedestal of admiration. Maintained a sterling silver reputation—except for one little spot of tarnish that can't be rubbed away but can be forgotten somehow, right? A little nuisance called a daughter, who was growing up in near poverty while you lived in luxury." The more Gray thought about the injustice, the angrier he got. "You say you made mistakes and made amends. I guess only for things the public could see. Frankly, I don't know how you sleep at night."

"Who—" Stuart stopped, swallowed. "Who is her mother?"

"Give me a break." Gray turned away.

Stuart grabbed his arm, forcing Gray to face him. "Who?"

His arm hurt where Stuart was crushing him. He refused to show it. "You know who. Karen Shaw."

"I don't know a Karen Sh—Simmons? Was her name Simmons before?"

"Simmons was her married name before she divorced. She took back her maiden name."

He dropped onto a chair, his head in his hands. "I met Karen when Marie and I were separated. We were both...wounded, and we lived together for two months. Her ex-husband had threatened her life, had already hurt her more than once. She needed a place to start over. I helped her, because she helped me to forgive myself and become a better man." He looked at Gray. "I gave her some money to help her get a new start. She said she would accept it only if I never contacted her again. I kept my end of the bargain. My marriage had been in shambles because of my guilt over your father's death."

Stuart looked around, at everything and at nothing. "Do you even know what that kind of guilt does to a man? I drank a lot. I made life miserable for Marie. She kicked me out, told me not to return until I could function again. Karen helped me to do that. But I didn't know there was a child. A child! I didn't know. I swear it. She never told me."

"How could you not know? Karen lived in the same damn city as you. No man—no decent man—would have an affair with a woman and not check back at least once to make sure he hadn't left her pregnant."

He looked up. "I asked her. I did. She told me she wasn't. I swear I didn't know. I wouldn't have abandoned her or her child." He finally looked his age. "I guess I always knew I would have to pay a price someday. Mollie. Does she know?"

"That you're her father? No. And I have no plans to tell her."

"You won't have a say in it."

"You accept what I'm saying, without proof?" Gray asked, knowing *he* wouldn't believe blindly, especially not a man out for vengeance.

"I imagine you have proof. The question is, how are you going to explain keeping the secret from her?"

The phone rang. Welcoming the interruption at the exact moment he was ready to grab Stuart by the throat, Gray controlled his voice as he answered, in case it was Mollie. "Hello?"

"Mr. McGuire, this is Ted at the front desk. Your wife just came running through the lobby, crying."

Fear slammed him in the gut. He pressed a hand to the wall. The baby—

"Has she gotten on the elevator yet?"

"No, sir. She was leaving the building."

Leaving the— No. God, no. Gray dropped the receiver into place and hurried to the front door. Wide-open. Accusingly open. On the floor lay a jumbled bouquet of carnations and a sack from Sheer Pleasure lingerie shop, something blue and lacy spilling out the top.

She must have come home during the heat of the argument and overheard them from behind the privacy wall.

In the worst way possible she'd learned that Stuart Fortune was her father.

Stuart came up beside him. "What's going on?" He knelt to pick up the items from the floor, then set them on the entry table.

"Mollie was here," Gray said flatly. "She obviously heard us talking and ran."

Stuart swore. "Ran where?"

Gray locked his hands behind his neck, trying to think past the panic that bubbled and boiled. *Stay focused.* Where would she go? Where would she go? "Maybe back to the shop. Maybe to Kelly's." He dropped his hands and looked around blindly. "She's pregnant. God. I don't know."

"You call the shop," Stuart said, taking command. "I'll call Kelly."

The authority in Stuart's voice jarred Gray into action. "I can find my own wife." He patted his pockets for his keys, then jogged out the door and down the hall to the elevator.

Following, Stuart pulled the door shut. "I have to do something."

A bell chimed; the down arrow flashed. "Just stay the hell out of the way."

"She won't harm herself, Gray. Or the baby."

The thought wouldn't have occurred to him in a million years. Of course she wouldn't.

Not on purpose.

He rushed into the elevator the minute the doors whooshed

open, punched the lobby button with his fist. "I don't need you telling me about my wife."

Stuart slipped in through the elevator doors before they shut. "I need to talk to her. To explain."

Gray watched the numbers count down until they reached the ground floor. He'd resisted looking at Stuart, afraid he would see a reflection of his own fear there. If Stuart was telling the truth, he was just as shocked as Mollie at the news. "I'll call you," he said, giving Stuart that much in case he was as innocent as he claimed to be, then he ran for the garage. His wife and child were out there somewhere, needing him. He wouldn't let them down.

At three o'clock in the morning Gray dragged himself back to the hotel. Alone. Kelly hadn't heard from her. He'd hung up the phone mid-tirade. Tasha knew something but wasn't talking. So he'd prowled the city, then widened his search to the country, checking out every hotel and motel along the route. His credit card company would alert him if she used it. Thank God there was some value in fame. People paid attention when he asked for favors. So far, however, the only charge she'd made was to Sheer Pleasure that afternoon, a whopping twenty-five dollars and fourteen cents.

He could understand her being shocked at learning she had a father, alive and well, but why had she run from Gray, too? She needed him now more than ever.

The phone rang. He snatched it up. "Mollie?"

"It's Tasha. I'm sorry."

"Is Mollie all right? God, please tell me she's all right."

"Look, Gray. I'm in the middle of whatever it is you're fighting about. I don't like it. First of all, she's not the type to run from something trivial. Second, she loves you with her whole heart. She needs some time. You need to give it to her."

"You know where she is."

"She's not with me, but she's safe. She hasn't told me what happened, though."

"I know what happened. What I can't figure out is why she's not talking to me. It wasn't my fault."

"Are you sure? She seems very angry at you."

"Why?"

"I figured you would know the answer to that. Anyway, get some sleep. She's okay where she is. No harm will come to her."

Why would Mollie be angry at him? "I need to hear her voice, Tasha. Do you think I could sleep? Do you? She's my world. Without her... Without her—" His throat closed up. Then a light came on, bright, blinding. He knew why she was mad at him. She'd not only discovered that Stuart was her father but that Gray had kept it from her.

She would see that as the ultimate betrayal, to keep such a secret. The realization seared him. Sweat beaded his forehead. His heart pounded. Why *would* she want to talk to him? Her husband? The person she was supposed to depend on the most? In trying to protect her, he'd destroyed her trust in him. To an unsuspecting soul like Mollie, such a violation would be punishable by...what?

He couldn't think of a consequence.

"Gray?"

He squeezed the telephone receiver. He'd forgotten Tasha was still on the line. "Help me find her," he said. "Please. I have to explain."

There was a long moment of silence, then, "I've heard that stress can ruin a person's health."

He tried to make sense of her words. Was she telling him something? Hope brought focus. "They say stress kills."

"Right. So, sometimes people need to get away for a while. Relax. Regroup. It doesn't even have to be far away. Sometimes closer is better, because you don't have to spend a lot of time traveling. I know that's my preference, anyway. Do you understand?"

He closed his eyes. "You have a getaway place. Mollie is there."

"All I'm saying is that she was very stressed. It's not good for her or the baby. I'm wondering just how good your computer skills are."

"Damn good." He needed to get busy. "Thank you, Tasha."

"Just set things right. That's all the thanks I need. And, Gray? We're even, okay?"

"More than even. 'Bye."

The minute he turned on the computer, he left an e-mail for Mollie in case she could check it somehow. Then he stared at the monitor, contemplating the illegal act he was about to perform. He'd only hacked into other computer systems to prove it could be done, to prove the need for security. Some codes were harder to break than others. But he needed to find his wife. He wouldn't sleep until she was home in his arms, where she belonged. They hadn't even made love in a week. He'd finally worked up the nerve to talk to her obstetrician, had just gotten back from there when Stuart called. The romantic evening he'd planned…

Swallowing the ache in his throat, he put his fingers on the keyboard and did what he knew best, grateful no one else had gotten their hands on his new encryption software—and consequences be damned.

Shortly after sunrise Gray pulled into the driveway of a small house nestled behind a thick shelter of trees and bushes, very near where they'd parked the night Mollie told him she was pregnant. At the end of the path sat her van.

Relief surged through him, paralyzing him for about fifteen seconds. He climbed out of the car and made his way to the door. He could hear the doorbell chime inside the house. He waited. After half a minute he rang again and knocked. Then he called her name.

Worried, he pressed his ear to the door. Nothing.

He banged louder. Yelled louder. Afraid, he moved around the house hammering his knuckles on each window, shouting her name. When he got to the front door again he didn't hesitate an instant. Terrified, he scooped up a planter and heaved it through the window alongside the door. Panicked, he reached inside to turn the lock, cutting himself on the jagged glass, leaving a trail of blood as he stormed from room to room.

In the last room he found a rumpled bed. Empty.

Fifteen

"I don't think this is a good idea," Mollie said, staring at an imposing two-story stone structure—Stuart's home—as he parked in the brick driveway. It was barely sunrise, yet lights were on in many of the rooms, not in welcome, Mollie feared, but in battle readiness.

She'd called Stuart in the early hours of the morning, and he'd come to see her at Tasha's vacation house. He told her that Marie now knew the whole story—or at least as much as he knew himself—and that he wanted Mollie to come home with him. His older son, Garrett, had flown in from Wyoming with his wife. His younger son, Jack, would drive over as soon as he was called. They would start becoming a family.

Brothers. She had brothers. She hadn't dared to hope—

"Delaying it serves no purpose, Mollie." Stuart turned off the engine and angled toward her. "Are you sure you don't want to call Gray?"

"Not yet." Her fury at her husband hadn't subsided. If anything, it had intensified.

"You can't hide from him forever." He held up a hand as

Mollie started to speak. "However, my first official act as your father will be to support you in whatever capacity you need."

"Are you sure your wife doesn't mind?" *I would be furious. Humiliated. Mortified.*

"Dad?"

A tall, handsome man approached the car, concern lining his face. Mollie almost burst into tears. Her brother, Garrett. Finally, officially, her brother, this rugged rancher from Wyoming. In the open doorway of the house stood a woman. Not Marie. Probably Renee, Garrett's wife. So many lives in upheaval. And it all could have been avoided. Damn Gray, she thought, more angry at him for making her swear, even if it was only in her mind.

Stuart opened his car door. Mollie followed suit, gathering her courage close. They were all going to hate her. She knew it. She was going to be worse off than before. She would have to run away to California— No, not there. Someplace, though, where she couldn't embarrass the family.

She swallowed the tears burning her throat at the silence around her. Garrett hated her. She could tell. He couldn't even say hello. "This is a mistake. Your family shouldn't be put through this," she said to Stuart, reaching for the door handle. "Please take me back."

Garrett moved then, slowly, steadily, until he stood before her. He put out his hand. "We met before, at Mac and Kelly's wedding. I'm Garrett." His gaze never wavered. "You have our father's eyes. So does Jack. Your other brother."

Her other brother. The words teased her composure, but she needed to stay in control. She still had to face Marie.

Mollie greeted Renee, who smiled with genuine welcome, then they all trooped into a formal living room that had a magnificent view of the lake. Marie awaited them, seated on a chair that looked like a throne to Mollie. She felt like Dorothy being presented to the great and powerful Wizard of Oz. Her knees wobbled. Someone came up beside her and cupped her elbow. Garrett. Her champion.

Stuart moved to stand beside Marie. "Introducing you seems ridiculous. You know each other."

"Hello, Mrs. Fortune." Mollie felt Garrett's grip tighten. She wouldn't faint. She wouldn't. "I wish I had something else to say. I don't." Her words drifted.

Marie looked at Stuart. "I've had the blue room prepared. She probably needs to rest. There's the baby to consider."

And if there wasn't, would you be yelling at me? Ordering me out? Blaming me? Mollie turned away, needing to disappear. "Yes. I would like to lie down for a while."

In the hall outside the living room, the phone rang.

"I'll get it," Renee said, hurrying out.

"It's probably Jack," Stuart said. "Tell him to come over anytime."

"How far along are you?" Garrett asked Mollie gently.

"Five weeks. Please," she whispered harshly. "Can you show me to my room? I need to be alone."

Renee stepped back in. "Stuart, it's someone from the police department who needs to speak to you."

Everyone froze in their positions until Stuart returned. He came up beside Mollie. "That was Gray, actually, calling to see if I'd heard from you. Also to say he's been arrested."

Mollie felt shockproof by now. "For what?"

"Breaking and entering."

"What?"

"Apparently he tracked you down to Tasha's place. He threw a planter through a window when he couldn't rouse you, which triggered a silent alarm."

Mollie pressed her fingers to her aching temples. "I'm married to a criminal."

Garrett smiled slightly. "I think you're married to a man who's out of his mind with worry."

"They're not charging him, Mollie, but I had to tell him I knew where you were, or else the police were going to get involved," Stuart said.

"I'm not ready to talk to him." Mollie almost growled the words.

"I didn't tell him you were here, only that you were fine and that he should give you a day," Stuart said. "Okay, here's the plan. Mollie will go upstairs and rest. We'll call the rest of the family, say we've got an announcement to make and have them all gather here this afternoon."

"So soon?" Mollie asked weakly.

He held her hands. "My dear, I think you'll find that the Fortunes are both resilient and staunchly loyal to their own. You'll be accepted in short order. You're innocent in all this."

Mollie glanced at Marie, who hadn't moved an inch the entire time Mollie had been in the room. How could she possibly be accepted when she would be a living reminder of her husband's affair?

"Mollie's dead on her feet," Renee said, sweeping in and taking over. "I'll show her to her room."

Mollie followed gratefully.

As dusk darkened the sky, Gray came to a stop at the entrance to Stuart's house. Electronic gates barred his entry. He had two choices—use the telephone at the gate to call and ask for admission, or climb the fence. He figured he had a better shot climbing the fence.

Just then the gates opened and a car emerged. He spotted Mason Chandler speeding away, then he aimed his car for the entrance. The gates started to close.... He winced as metal scraped metal, but kept going, stopping behind a long row of cars. A party? They were having a party?

Gray caught a glimpse of himself in the rearview mirror. He hadn't shaved in thirty-six hours. Or showered. Or changed clothes. But after exhausting every other possibility, he had decided to force Stuart's hand. Gray had spent the day at the computer trying to find where Mollie could be hiding. He'd turned up plenty of information on the Fortune family but nothing that led him to his wife.

Afraid of being barred from entry, and figuring that a trespassing arrest wouldn't hurt him any more than the breaking and entering charge, Gray tried the handle on the front door. Unlocked. He crept in, then followed the sound of voices tumbling over each other. "I can't believe Chloe would break off the engagement." "Do you think she really ran away?" "Of course Mason will find her."

Gray stood just outside the door to the roomful of people. Had they all gathered just because Chloe Fortune had apparently broken her engagement and run off? Chloe wasn't Stuart's child, but Emmet's—the other side of the family. A moment of longing passed through Gray as he wished for that kind of family support. He and Mollie would start building that—as soon as he found her and they talked this situation out.

He peered around the doorway. Everyone was talking—except Mollie. He pulled out of sight, leaned against the wall for support. *Mollie.* Safe. Anger followed on the heels of relief. Stuart had lied to him, undoubtedly with Mollie's consent.

After a minute he looked into the room again. His wife was standing between her half brothers, Jack and Garrett, like a protected little sister. Who the hell did she need protection from, anyway? Him?

He finger combed his hair, tucked in his shirt and stepped through the doorway. Quiet spread across the room like one domino toppling another in slow motion. Ignoring her guards, he stopped in front of his wife.

"Are you all right?" he asked.

Mollie dug her fingers into her palms. Oh, he looked awful. So unlike him. "What happened to your hand?"

He looked at the bandage as if he'd forgotten it. "Nothing. We need to talk. Alone."

"You don't have to do anything you don't want to," Garrett said to Mollie. "You choose the timetable."

"Stay the hell out of this, Fortune," Gray said distinctly. "Mollie, please. We can't hash out our personal problems in public."

"This is her family," Jack said. "Not the public."

Mollie locked gazes with Gray. He begged her with his eyes. Begged her. He had always been the epitome of patience and kindness with her, but he looked like a wild man now, unshaven and disheveled. She knew the turmoil inside herself wouldn't settle down, either, until they had spoken.

"Is there a room where we could speak privately?" she asked Stuart, who had joined the small group.

"Yes, of course. Come this way." He led them out the door

and down the hall to a room Mollie figured was called a library. Books lined the walls.

Stuart glanced from Mollie to Gray, then back again. "You've both been through a lot. You're both tired. Take that into consideration here." Then he left, his fatherly advice dispensed, his confidence in Gray indicated by the fact he shut the door behind him.

"Are you all right?" Gray asked, taking a step toward her.

She retreated.

He stopped.

"I'm fine."

"Mollie, please sit down. The baby—"

"Is fine, too. And I choose to stand." She folded her arms across her stomach. "I can't believe you got yourself arrested."

"Even if I'd stopped to considered I was breaking any laws, it wouldn't have stopped me. Your car was there. You didn't answer the door. I yelled at every window. What else could I do? I thought you were hurt. Or unconscious. Or…worse." He shoved his hands through his hair and walked away from her. "I thought you might be losing the baby." The words came out low and hoarse. "I was afraid."

The emotion was genuine and heartfelt, Mollie knew that. But it didn't let him off the hook. "If privacy is such a big issue with you, as you told me once, how is it you knew that Stuart was my father?"

"Ah. First things first, I guess." He turned to face her. "The information pretty much dropped into my lap while I was researching Knight Star and how I could get it. I wasn't looking to dig up any dirt on Stuart. I never expected there was any."

"Why didn't you tell me?"

Mirroring her pose, he crossed his arms. "In the beginning I was going to. My original plan was to join forces with you against him. Expose him for the fraud he was. Then I met you, and I knew I couldn't ask that of you. And then, I— We got married. You had me, then. You didn't need him." Again he took a step toward her; again she retreated. "I'm sorry you found out about him by overhearing it. I was certain Stuart had abandoned you, that he had paid your mother for her silence."

She shook her head, again and again.

"Yes," Gray insisted. "You were a symbol of his fall from grace."

"You're wrong. You're so wrong about everything. Everything." She sought refuge at the window, needing the peace of the quiet setting, but barely aware of it. "Stuart didn't know, but I did. I did."

A mantel clock ticked in the silence. "That's impossible," Gray said at last.

"Why?"

"Because you couldn't keep something like that to yourself."

"Why? Because I'm young? Naive? I may be both of those, but I'm not a home wrecker."

"No. Because family is so important to you. You had a father. Brothers. I can't picture you not telling them. How long have you known?"

She rubbed her face with her hands. "Since shortly after my mother's death. I agonized over what to do. I wanted to tell him. I desperately wanted to." *But at the baby shower Marie said she would murder her husband if she ever found out he strayed.* "But I made the decision not to complicate his life. I had been welcomed into the Fortune family when Kelly married Mac, and I was working with them, but they were also becoming my friends. I thought it was enough. I had the flower shop, the shop my mother bought with Stuart's money. My legacy."

"I thought you were a victim. Like me."

"A victim of what? I didn't lack for anything. My mother loved me enough for two. She provided for me. I couldn't have asked for more." The rest of his words registered. "How were you a victim?"

"It doesn't matter now." He came up beside her. They gazed out the window together, the silence thick. "Nothing matters but you and the baby. I'm so sorry. I didn't know."

She rounded on him, letting loose with the bottled-up anger. "Ignorance doesn't absolve you. What you did was unconscionable. You should have told me what you knew, discussed it with me, your wife, the mother of your unborn child. I trusted you enough to marry you without any declaration of love on your part. You didn't trust me the tiniest bit.''

"Seems to me that we both had secrets.''

"I was still getting used to the idea.'' She had to sit down, after all. "Most of the time I could block it from my mind. I didn't even know about Knight Star, because I was afraid to know too much about him. I thought that the more I knew, the more tempted I would be to tell him. Maybe that's something you couldn't do. But I had to. It was only hard when I was in the same room as Stuart.''

Mollie sat in a chair, keeping a huge, formidable desk between her and Gray. "You were threatening to take over his company, which would have destroyed my relationship with the Fortunes—my family but not my family. I would have told you before I let you do that. According to my mother's journal, Stuart is a kind, wonderful man who anguished over causing another man's death. I didn't need to bring more pain into his life.''

Gray blew out a breath. "That man was—''

"I don't see how we can stay married,'' she said, sadness flowing through her, a river of loss after having found an ocean of love. "Not without trust, and especially not without love. I trusted you a lot. A lot. And just as soon as you loved me, I would've trusted you completely. I had to keep something in reserve, don't you see? I had to. And I was right to! Our relationship was fragile before this, and now it's cracked. I don't know how to patch it, Gray.''

"We can fix it. Let me explain.''

"You married me for all the wrong reasons. You don't respect me. I'm your possession or something. I tried to be patient. I tried to make you fall in love with me. Nothing worked. We can stay married until the baby is born, then—''

"No!'' Gut punched, Gray shot forward, desperation gathering like a funnel cloud inside him. He leaned over the desk. "No divorce.''

"I don't see another solution.''

"You're not looking hard enough. You're tired. Tomorrow you'll feel better. We'll talk. Everything will work out.''

"It won't change anything.''

She was going to leave him. She'd said she loved him. Again and again, she'd said so. Her guarantee for life. No matter what.

No matter what. Her love was supposed to be unconditional, just like— Damn it. Damn it all to hell and back. He was going to be alone again, with no one to kiss good night. No one to take care of. They'd made a baby together. He was supposed to give all that up because he'd hurt her without meaning to? That was love, to give up so easily? He was glad he hadn't told her he loved her. Glad. At least she couldn't hold that over his head. He'd let down his guard once, had begun to believe he had truly found happiness. He wouldn't be suckered into that again.

He fought back, his voice as cool as he could make it. "You signed the prenuptial agreement, which clearly states that if we have a child, there will be no divorce. I intend to hold you to every clause."

Her face went white. "I can't believe you would force me to keep to that stupid agreement I signed without reading."

"I told you to read it."

"I asked you if there was anything written in it that a lawyer of mine would object to! You only mentioned money, which you knew didn't matter to me. You see! This is just another example of why we can't stay married. And I'm sure it's a legality I can circumvent. Maybe I can't get a divorce, but I don't have to move back home with you. I can stay with my family."

Gray staggered back a step. Her family? He was her family. And the baby they made together. And all the ones yet to come. How could he tell her? What words would make the difference? Words of love? If he said them now, she would throw them back in his face.

He touched her hand. She jerked it away. That hurt more than anything. He'd finally discovered he could touch and not be rebuffed. Another lesson learned. "You're mine," he said, the words roaring out like thunder. "Mine." He moved around the desk, pulled her into his arms and kissed her, knowing he was hurting her, not knowing any other way of showing her how he felt.

God. What had he become? He had to leave, before he hurt her even more. "I'm sorry, Mollie." He hoped he said it aloud.

He left the room, the house, the property. Walk, hurry, jog, run. Faster. Don't let her see you like this. Don't let her know how you feel. Out of breath, he slid into his car, revved the engine, peeled rubber down the brick driveway, the gates opening magically just as he reached them. He drove mindlessly, stupidly, worse than a drunk who didn't know what he was doing, because he knew. He knew.

Mollie. Mollie. Her name spilled from his heart, from his throat. You said you loved me. You said.

He was going to kill someone if he kept driving. Maybe himself—

No. Not himself. He wasn't a coward. Nothing was that bad. Nothing. He still had a child to think of. A wife to win back. Life to live.

He slowed down, finding himself at the spot overlooking the lake where they'd parked just last week and got caught necking. He stared at the water. Memories came and went.

Twenty-five years of grief spilled out of him. He fought giving in to it for as long as he could. Then he put his head against the steering wheel and, for the first time since he was eight, he cried.

She had a shoulder to cry on. Mollie let Stuart comfort her as she cried, her heart broken. "How can I love a man like that?" she asked Stuart, who had come into the library seconds after Gray left. "If he has any emotions at all, they're buried so deep he could never dig a path to them. And I still love him!"

"Remember what he's been through, too, Mollie. His father's suicide devastated—"

"What!" She shoved herself back. "Suicide? What are you talking about?"

"You don't know?"

"Obviously I don't. Tell me."

He took her hand, then led her to the sofa. "Do you even know who his father was, honey?"

She shook her head. "He never speaks of him."

"His name was Charlie Knight."

"Knight? So, Knight Star Systems—"

"Charlie's company. I won't give you all the details now, but after I took over the company, Charlie committed suicide. Soon after, Gretchen left town, taking Gray with her. No one ever heard from her again. She seemed to just disappear. When Gray showed up here, he wasn't using the name Knight. I didn't put it together. None of us did. Even Mason, for all his digging, didn't come up with that."

Mollie stopped listening. Suicide. "I have to go see him," she said, stopping his monologue of explanation. "I have to go right now. I don't have a car. I need a car." She stood, swayed.

Stuart grabbed her. "You're not going anywhere other than to bed. There'll be plenty of time in the morning to deal with this."

"But I didn't know about his father. It explains so much!"

"Nothing will change between now and the morning."

"I wouldn't listen to him! I have to listen—"

"Not tonight. Think of the baby, Mollie. You need to rest first."

Exhaustion made her dizzy. It was all too much for her. The pregnancy, being revealed to the Fortune family, the tension of meeting everyone, enduring Marie's stoic acceptance of Mollie's presence in the house. Then Gray's vow that he would hold her to the prenuptial agreement. And now, the way his father died.

After she climbed into bed, she stared at the telephone beside her. She wished she had her computer. They always talked so freely on e-mail. But even as the thought occurred to her, she found oblivion in sleep.

Mollie didn't expect anyone to be up at 5:00 a.m., but she couldn't stay in bed another second. She crept down the stairs and hunted until she found the kitchen, then came to a stop when she saw Marie standing at the counter pouring a cup of coffee.

"I'm sorry," Mollie mumbled, retreating.

"Don't go, Mollie." She held up the pot. "Would you like some?"

"No, thank you. Some crackers, though," she said hesitantly.

"Morning sickness?"

"It just started a few days ago. Crackers help."

"Have a seat. I'll get you some."

Mollie watched her move to a cupboard and lift down a box. She put a few on a plate, then set them in front of Mollie. "Thanks."

"Anything else?"

"This is fine." She took a bite.

"You've had a rough time."

Tears sprang to Mollie's eyes. Her throat closed. She nodded.

"Marriage is never simple. Someone should tell us during the ceremony that it's one big roller-coaster ride. Whatever our expectations are, they get shattered with surprising frequency, at least early on. Eventually things settle down. Then just when you think you've gotten onto the merry-go-round instead, you're in line for the roller coaster again."

Was she trying to say she had accepted her? Mollie wondered. Or that Mollie was a scary amusement park ride?

The kitchen door opened. Stuart came in. His gaze moved from Mollie to Marie, who attempted a smile.

"Everything okay in here?" he asked.

"Come sit down, please, Stuart," Marie said. "I need to talk to both of you."

Mollie's stomach got queasier. She bit into another cracker.

"I asked Stuart to sleep in another room last night. It was the first time we had slept apart under the same roof. Stuart thinks it was because I was having trouble dealing with learning about you, Mollie."

Mollie shifted her gaze to Stuart, noted the frown on his face, then focused on Marie again.

"The truth is," Marie said, "I was dealing with my own guilt. You see, I've known about you all along."

Stuart's face darkened as Marie looked at him squarely.

"Did you really think I was going to give you up? I loved you. We had sons to consider, too. They were young. Thirteen and eight. I didn't want them to be without a father. So I waited you out, hoping you would come back, but needing to know what I was fighting."

"You knew I had a daughter and you didn't tell me?"

"I wasn't positive. I knew you'd had an affair. I knew she was pregnant soon after. The timing was right. I didn't want to believe it, so I didn't." She looked at Mollie, who didn't know how she felt about anything anymore. "I've been waiting for you to claim him. I watched you at Mac and Kelly's wedding. Your eyes kept drifting to Stuart and Jack and Garrett. There was such hunger there. I knew then that I'd been right all along. I also knew that you knew Stuart was your father. I waited for you to tell him, but you kept it to yourself. I admired that. I also despised you for it, for the fresh guilt it planted in me. You made an enormously mature decision."

"I was honoring my mother's wishes. Oh! I'm sorry—"

"It's all right. And you will always be welcome here. As Stuart said, you are innocent in all this." She took Stuart's hand. "We both have something to forgive. It may take you more time, because what I did was worse. I should've confronted you, so we could have dealt with it then. I hope eventually—"

Stuart drew her into his arms as a tear spilled down her cheek.

"I'll leave you alone," Mollie said.

Just then the door opened and Garrett walked in.

"Gray's here, Mollie. He wants to talk to you."

She pressed a hand to her stomach. "He's up early."

"He doesn't look like he went to bed."

Mollie didn't want to feel sympathy for him. Or concern. Or love. But it was all beyond her control. She couldn't shut off her emotions like he could.

"There's a pretty little gazebo overlooking the lake," Marie said. "Stuart and I have solved a lot of problems there."

Be fearless. Gray's words came back to her, at first in a whisper, then in a deep-throated shout that echoed on and on. He should've taken his own advice.

Her scent reached him first, then her voice.

"Hi."

A simple hello. Music to his ears. He was afraid she wouldn't talk to him at all.

Turning around, he watched her walk toward him, crumbling

inside, longing to beg for forgiveness, knowing that wouldn't be enough. He clenched his fists against the need to pull her into his arms and never let her go.

"You look terrible," she said, examining him.

"Should've seen me before I showered and shaved. I would've scared off trick-or-treaters."

"Did you sleep?"

"The bed was too big." He reached inside his jacket and pulled out a manila envelope, then passed it to her.

She took it without comment, clutched it to her chest. "Let's go for a walk."

As they stepped out the front door he took off his jacket and laid it over her shoulders. She ducked her head, but pulled the garment tighter to her. He'd never seen her so quiet. It scared the hell out of him.

"Why didn't you tell me about your father?" she asked at last.

He focused on the morning, on the gentle birdsong, on the crisp scent of wood smoke. Autumn at its glorious best. "It's a poor excuse, but I didn't know how to put it into words. I lived on his memory, was driven by it. If I gave it up, I would have given up a big part of my life."

"I thought about you most of the night," she said. "About how he died. About how much you lost. You must be so angry at him, to have kept it locked up inside like that."

"I didn't realize how angry until last night. He abandoned me. Took the coward's way out. Then he left me to deal with the mess he left behind. I thought he loved me. That doesn't equate to love."

"Of course he loved you. But he didn't have your strength. He didn't know that life is too precious to throw it away because he'd made some mistakes. People can start over. They just need time and help."

"I forgave him, Mollie. Last night, in the darkest hour of my life, I found a way to forgive him."

Still she didn't look at him. "That's a big step for you."

"It seems so small now, in comparison."

"To what?"

"Losing you."

They reached the gazebo and stepped inside but didn't sit, standing instead, side by side, looking out at the lake.

"What's in the envelope?" she asked.

"The prenuptial agreement."

"You're going to hold me to it?" Her voice shook. "You want me to stay because of some piece of paper?"

"Look inside, Mollie. It's torn in half. I invalidated it. You'll stay only if you want to. I hope you want to."

"I need a tissue," she said suddenly, dropping the envelope to a bench, fumbling in his jacket pockets.

"I'm sorry. I don't have—"

She held up the Popsicle stick. Finally she looked at him. The sheen in her eyes made his throat convulse.

"Why did you keep this?" she asked.

"It was an impulse. Then it became a connection when I wasn't with you." He took it from her, touched it to his lips, then hers. "First kiss."

"I found it in your nightstand," she admitted. "It gave me hope."

"Speaking of hope…" He dug into his shirt pocket and pulled out one of her birthday candles. "I reread them last night. I'm sorry if I intruded, but I thought you'd shared them all. I didn't realize you hadn't. This one caught me off guard."

Mollie read the words from her twentieth birthday: "I wish a true and honest man would fall in love with me."

"No red star," he said, touching the paper, then running his finger across hers.

She shook her head, but she didn't pull away.

"I want to grant you that wish. I can give you half already. I know I have to earn the other half." Gray took a chance and held her hand. Her fingers clamped around his. Her face contorted, fighting new tears. "I love you, Mollie. I love you with all my heart. I'll be that true and honest man, if you'll give me a chance. I'll undo everything I've done to Stuart's company. I'll fix anything, do anything, be anything, if you'll just love me again and stay with me. I want to be a family with you."

Tears spilled down her face. He brushed them away. "I don't

deserve you, but I'm begging you. Please don't leave me. You told me once that you thought fate brought us together. I knew I'd maneuvered the meeting—and yet you had those pictures that you claimed had brought you out of mourning, even before we met."

"Not a claim. The truth!"

"You handed me such an awesome responsibility, never to disappoint you. I didn't live up to it. Do you think you can ever forgive me? Will you let me try again? I'll do anything for you."

"Just love me," she said, putting his hand on her abdomen. "Us."

Joy spilled from him, trouncing his fears, banishing his pain. "My beautiful, beautiful Mollie. That's the easy part," he said, kissing her, claiming her forever. He'd caught the leprechaun, after all, and the treasure was priceless. Her scent drifted around him, but he didn't have to wonder anymore what to call it. It had a name—heaven.

*   *   *   *   *

*Find out what happens between Chloe Fortune
and Mason Chandler in*

Undercover Groom
by
Merline Lovelace

Available now.

For a sneak preview turn the page…

This time, Chloe Fortune vowed she wouldn't wimp out.

This time, she'd either sweep everything off Mason's burled-mahogany desk and make wild, uninhibited love to him on its polished surface or... She gulped. Or she'd hand him back the four-carat emerald-cut solitare he'd slipped on her ring finger last January.

Last January! She paused with her hand on the brass door latch, thinking of her unconventional engagement. She couldn't quite believe that she and Mase had been engaged for almost nine months. Or that they'd shared only a few casual kisses in all that time.

Okay, so maybe their self-imposed restraint had been part of the ground rules she'd laid down when she proposed to Mase. After all, she was the one who'd come up with the phony engagement in the first place. At the time it had seemed like the perfect answer to her dilemma.

She'd known Mase Chandler off and on for most of her life, first as her older brother Mac's best friend and then as her occasional escort. Their phony engagement had worked perfectly...at first. She just wasn't quite sure when or how the engagement had taken on a life of its own. And she couldn't pinpoint the exact moment she'd realized she wanted her *fake* engagement to be a *real* wedding.

She only knew she missed Mase when he was gone on one of his long, extended business trips. That the hand he planted in the small of her back to guide her to a table burned right through whatever she was wearing. That she ached to peel off his hand-tailored suit, unknot his tie, unbutton his shirt and plant hot, greedy kisses all over his naked chest.

All of which she fully intended to do today.

If she didn't lose her nerve!

They couldn't continue the deception any longer. Chloe either had to call the engagement off...or convince Mase to toss out the original ground rules and make wild, reckless love to her.

He wanted to. For all his deliberate restraint, Chloe sensed the desire he so carefully kept in check. She'd tried to hint that she was ready...more than ready!...for him to unleash it. This time, she vowed, she'd do more than just hint.

Dragging in a deep, steadying breath, Chloe pushed down the brass latch. The heavy oak door slid open noiselessly. She'd taken only a single step when the sound of a husky contralto floated across the luxurious office suite.

"Come on, Mase. You love what we do together. Surely you're not going to give it up just because you're engaged?"

Mase was leaning against the front edge of his desk. Beneath his neat black hair, his tanned face bore a smile that ripped at Chloe's heart. His hands rested on the brunette's waist, while hers played with his tie. The same silk tie that Chloe had envisioned slowly unknotting just seconds ago!

"No, I'm not giving it up because I'm engaged. I told you my reasons."

"None of which will matter when the fireworks start," his companion purred, tickling the underside of his jaw with the tie ends. "You're hooked, just like I am. You crave the thrill, the excitement of our little game."

His smile tipped into a wry grin. "I don't think you can call what we do a game, Pam. We've taken it too close to the edge too many times."

"And that's what makes it so wonderful. What makes us so damned good together. No one plays it harder or faster or rougher than you do."

Chloe choked. She didn't want to hear any more. Now she understood why Mase hadn't taken her up on her subtle hints about morphing their pretend relationship into a real one. Misery and fury she had no right to feel coursed through her. She must have made some movement, some sudden jerk, because the brunette flicked a quick look over Mase's shoulder.

Another man might have stammered or flushed in embarrassment at being caught in such intimacy by his supposed fiancée. Not Mase. Not calm, controlled, always-in-command Mase.

"I'm sorry, Chloe. I didn't know you were here."

"Obviously not."

"Please, come in. I'd like you to meet Pam Hawkins. She's a business associate of mine."

He didn't blush. Didn't even blink. Chloe had to fight the hurt and fury tearing through her. She had no right to feel this awful jealousy, she reminded herself fiercely. Mase hadn't made her any promises. He was a friend. Only a friend.

The realization made her even more miserable.

"I'm sorry I disturbed you."

"You didn't. We've finished our business."

"You're finished? Strange. From where I'm standing, it looked as though you were just getting started. I'll talk to you another time. When you're not quite so busy."

"I'm sorry you walked in on that. It's not what it seems... I can't believe I just said that."

"You don't have to explain anything. Not anymore. As of this moment you're a free man, Mase. Officially, finally and irrevocably," Chloe said, walking outside to the elevator.

"I'm not letting you walk away until we talk this through," Mase said, catching up to her as the elevator opened and she got in.

"I can't talk about it now. I don't *want* to talk about it now."

Finally the door whirred shut. Chloe slumped against the paneled wall, her eyes shut, but Mase's image blazed on her eyelids Tall. Dark-haired. Broad-shouldered. Square-jawed. Smiling down at Pamela Hawkins, who liked it hard and fast and rough.

A shiver of revulsion ripped through Chloe, followed immediately by one of pure, undiluted envy. Mase Chandler hadn't tried anything hard and fast and rough with her. Face it. He hadn't tried anything at all. It shattered her even more to realize that she still wanted him. Desperately.

* * *

Don't forget Undercover Groom
by Merline Lovelace is on the shelves now!

Sometimes bringing up baby can bring surprises –and showers of love! For the cutest and cuddliest heroes and heroines, choose the Special Edition™ book marked

That's my baby!

Welcome back to the drama and mystery that is the Fortune Dynasty.

A Fortune's Children Wedding is coming to you at a special price of only £3.99 and contains a money off coupon for issue one of *Fortune's Children Brides*.

With issue one priced at a special introductory offer of 99p you can get it **FREE** with your money off coupon.

▼™ SILHOUETTE
SPECIAL EDITION®

AVAILABLE FROM 19TH MAY 2000

SHE'S HAVING HIS BABY Linda Randall Wisdom

That's My Baby!

Jake Roberts was everything Caitlin O'Hara wanted in her baby's father—he was fun, warm and gorgeous. They'd shared every intimate detail of their lives since childhood. Why not a baby?

A FATHER'S VOW Myrna Temte

Montana

Sam Brightwater wanted to start a traditional family. So the *last* woman he should be attracted to was Julia Stedman, who was only sampling her heritage. But Julia got under his skin and soon they were making love and making a baby…

BETH AND THE BACHELOR Susan Mallery

Beth was a suburban mother of two and her friends had set her up with a blind date—millionaire bachelor Todd Graham! He was sexy, eligible—everything a woman could want…

BUCHANAN'S PRIDE Pamela Toth

Leah Randall took in the man without a memory, but she had no idea who he was. They never planned to fall in love, not when he could be anyone…even one of her powerful Buchanan neighbours!

THE LONG WAY HOME Cheryl Reavis

Rita Warren had come home. She had things to prove. She didn't need a troublemaking soldier in her already complicated life. But 'Mac' McGraw was just impossible to ignore.

CHILD MOST WANTED Carole Halston

Susan Gulley had become a mother to her precious orphaned nephew, but she hadn't banked on falling for his handsome but hard-edged uncle. What would Jonah do when he learned the secret she'd been keeping?

Diana Palmer

THE TEXAS RANGER
He has a passion for justice

Published 15th March 2002

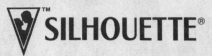

MAN OF THE MONTH

Look out for Desire's™ hottest hunks! Every month we feature our most sensual and sizzling man in a specially marked book.

SILHOUETTE DESIRE